THE SECRET
OF THE
STORYTELLER

A Novel

EM RICHTER

BALBOA
PRESS

A DIVISION OF HAY HOUSE

Balboa Press books may be ordered through booksellers or by contacting:

Balboa Press
A Division of Hay House
1663 Liberty Drive
Bloomington, IN 47403
www.balboapress.com
1-(877) 407-4847

Because of the dynamic nature of the Internet, any web addresses or links contained in this book may have changed since publication and may no longer be valid. The views expressed in this work are solely those of the author and do not necessarily reflect the views of the publisher, and the publisher hereby disclaims any responsibility for them.

The author of this book does not dispense medical advice or prescribe the use of any technique as a form of treatment for physical, emotional, or medical problems without the advice of a physician, either directly or indirectly. The intent of the author is only to offer information of a general nature to help you in your quest for emotional and spiritual well-being. In the event you use any of the information in this book for yourself, which is your constitutional right, the author and the publisher assume no responsibility for your actions.

Book cover design by Lucinda Kinch

Any people depicted in stock imagery provided by Thinkstock are models, and such images are being used for illustrative purposes only. Certain stock imagery © Thinkstock.

ISBN: 978-1-4525-7624-4 (sc)
ISBN: 978-1-4525-7626-8 (hc)
ISBN: 978-1-4525-7625-1 (e)

Library of Congress Control Number: 2013910571

Printed in the United States of America.
Balboa Press rev. date: 08/20/2013

*To Daniel, for keeping my feet on the ground,
and to Aidan, Liam and Ella
for giving me the greatest of all gifts.*

PROLOGUE

Thursday night, September 29th, 2000
Old City of Jerusalem

"Who are you looking for?" the old woman uttered as she opened the door. I didn't know what to answer her.

The yells and cries continued in the street. A cacophony of voices. Chaos in action. Screams of injustice in a language I didn't understand.

Please let me in, please let me in, let me in, I silently screamed, my voice betraying me.

The old woman's wizened eyes twinkled as they smiled from behind the veil of soft eyelids. I stood in the doorway, desperate to leave the dark, winding streets behind. I wanted to run to her and hide, to have the old woman protect me. I wanted the solace of her home. I wanted refuge.

In the time I'd been searching for her, I'd never thought of what I would say to her. Now here I was, in the foyer in front of her apartment, and I couldn't say a thing. I just wanted to feel safe, hidden from the outside world.

"I'm looking for, um…Natalie told me…I followed the birds. I was looking for a place…" I glanced at the shadows behind me, realizing just how ridiculous I must sound.

What if I'd gotten it all wrong?

What if the signs were merely my imagination?

What if this wasn't the home of the old woman—the one they called La Que Saba?

What if La Que Saba didn't exist after all?

"Ah, my little bird, your questions remind me of the story of the If Sisters." She didn't move from the entryway. As she spoke, her gaze drifted from me to some far off point above my eyes and back again. Her voice was soothing, soft and caressing, like a gentle ripple of wind on my skin. Her accent turned each word into a longer version of itself.

"The sisters were called What-If, If-Yes and If-No. Just like you, they never tired of their questions. Just like you, they would not trust anything they knew to be true. Just like you, they danced the dance of doubt." Her gaze held mine. "They were born of the seed of Fate and the womb of Chance. Beautiful were those sisters. Captivating. How they danced! They would hypnotize all who watched them. Always the same dance, the same steps, the same rhythm. What-If would start, If-Yes would twirl, If-No would turn. As the waves of the sea crashed to meet the shore, the sisters continued to eternity. Questions were asked, answers were given, but the Sisters still twirled and turned in their Ifs. The Sisters danced in a circle of questions until they were mad. And Fate and Chance mourned their daughters who asked the questions but never accepted the answers."

She looked at me for a long moment and then continued. "Fate and Chance came to you, little bird. But all you saw were the mad sisters dancing in front of your eyes, confusing your mind with their hypnotic dance. Fate never abandoned you. Chance came to you to guide your way."

She held the door open and gestured inside, but before I walked through, I looked behind me once more. In the dark, I could see the faint shadow of the *bulbul* perched on the top of the gate.

In the distance someone yelled words of war.

Someone screamed for retaliation.

Someone shot a single bullet in the air.

The *bulbul* flew away.

I stepped into safety.

Part I

THE GIFT OF WISDOM

Wisdom went forth to dwell among the sons of men,
But she obtained not habitation.
Wisdom found not a place on earth where she could inhabit;
Her dwelling, therefore, is in Heaven
Book of Enoch

Chapter 1

Wednesday September 28th, 2000
Somewhere over the Atlantic

The purpose of a story, any story, is to give order to reality. Not just chronological order, but also degrees of importance. But, although they are never linear, by their very nature, stories must involve a beginning, middle and an end. Life rarely affords us such a clear view. We are not privy to the view of a new epoch while standing at the very precipice of that new era. We are unaware of the transformation that we are about to undergo until later, often much later. But a story is a seed that must be planted in order to grow.

I could have chosen to plant the seed of this story in my childhood, with the endearing voice that comes from childish innocence and truth, the cross-country moves, the story of my unusual upbringing, if only I could remember it. Or, I would have started at the obvious beginning, with the mystery of my conception, the intrigue of those lost early years, but that would be flavorless. I could have chosen to begin with my mother's sickness, the hospital, her funeral, my debt, the sorrow. But, that is not the story I want to tell. Maybe I should have planted this story in the rich earth of the years that have passed since the day

I met the woman who changed my life. But, that would tell of the soil and not of the seed.

The seed of my story was planted in flight.

Tall and slender, bringing with her a smell of lavender soap and patchouli incense, she glided towards the back galley and seemed to take up the whole space. She could have been mistaken for a famous actress, lean, leggy and untamed. She reminded me of a young colt, unbridled and wild, the kind that roamed free in the fields behind our community in California, where my mother and I lived for a spring and summer when I was a child. Not the newborn colts because they stayed close to their mothers, but the ones just learning to break free, the unpredictable ones. I was both entranced and intimidated by her.

Three hours into the flight and we were already chasing the night. The passengers were all nestled comfortably in their seats, and the aisles were dark except for the light from the galley. As she approached, I stood up, my jump seat thwacking against the wall as it closed behind me. She tilted her head to me and smiled, her lips glistening with pale pink gloss.

"Can I get you a coffee?" I offered.

"I'd love one. Black."

Her skin was sun-kissed and smooth, and she looked at me through green eyes framed by thick, black lashes. She wore a long blue beach dress, dangling earrings and jingling bangles. Despite the eclectic mix, she was chicly bohemian. Her long, dark hair cascaded down her back.

"I guess we're together for the next few hours," she said in a throaty and surprisingly smooth voice. As she ran one hand through her long hair and pushed the straggling strands behind one ear, her bangles made little tambourine clinks.

I felt the weight of my self-doubt rise. The fabric of my uniform was suffocating, and the belt was pinching into my waist. The red polyester ascot became a chain around my neck. My movements felt stiff, clunky and mechanical compared to her graceful, light gestures. Next to her radiant skin, I sensed the hue of my face become sallow. My brown, curly hair, pulled into a tight bun at the nape of my neck, was constricting compared to the free sway and bounce of this bohemian woman. *Fuck, Selena, stop feeling so sorry for yourself.*

There were a few quiet hours between the dinner and breakfast service, hours within which I had planned to read my book and research it for my paper. It was the beginning of the semester, my first month of trying to juggle college courses with what was turning out to be more than just a summer job with the airline. But the juggling act was proving to be more difficult than I'd expected.

The real problem, I was coming to realize, was that people loved to talk to the flight attendants in the middle of a flight. Galley therapy, we called it. Given the chance, people would spend hours talking about themselves, telling stories of their lives, their travels, troubles and children. Always commenting on what a good listener I was, but really, they were just thankful to have anyone to talk with. Any listener would do. That's the trick to being a good listener—if I simply let people talk about themselves, they always would.

Now this woman was standing in the galley smiling at me, wanting to talk, keeping me from my studies. I politely looked

5

away. I glanced behind her, brought my gaze down to my lap, fidgeted with some napkins, rearranged the headphones, checked the coffee pots and picked an invisible hangnail from my thumb. I put my book on the counter. All the while, I could feel the bohemian beauty staring at me. She wasn't getting the hint. Finally, I let my eyes meet her gaze.

The beauty smiled, revealing a perfect, white row of teeth. I smiled back with closed lips as my tongue swept across my upper teeth.

"Are you reading 'The Return of the Goddess'? It's one of my favorites."

"You know it?" I picked up the book, a last minute purchase from the campus bookshop. It was one of the many choices of required reading I had to write an essay on, due that Monday. It was the last book I would have chosen, but it was all that was left in stock. I'd been too late to attend the group study and too busy to study it at home. Now I was feeling the pressure of my hectic schedule.

"Actually, I'm not exactly reading it. I'm researching it for an assignment," I admitted.

"Are you a student?"

"Trying to be." I shrugged. "I'm majoring in cultural anthropology. First year."

"Oh, a fellow story lover." She offered her outstretched hand. "I'm Natalie. Natalie Rose."

"I'm Selena Silver. Nice to meet you."

Her handshake was surprisingly firm; yet, her hand was delicate, the skin, smooth and soft, and the nails perfectly manicured and shockingly red.

"Are you going to Tel Aviv for long, Selena?" she asked.

"My layover is until Friday night. You?"

"I'm just landing there and then going straight to Jerusalem. I'm going to do a little research myself." She winked, as if including me in on a little secret.

"Research? What are you researching?"

"Well," she turned her head slightly, as if assessing who may be listening. Sure that no one was around, she leaned closer and continued at no more than a murmur, "To be more exact, I'm not researching, but searching." She smiled and straightened up.

"What exactly are you searching for?" The question tumbled out of my mouth before I had a chance to catch it. The last thing I wanted was to start a whole conversation, but something about this enigmatic woman compelled me to ask. Something about her made me curious, the type of curiosity I rarely felt around people, who were mostly self-absorbed in their own troubles. My preference was for fantasy people, characters in books who lived life in a much more miraculous way.

She sipped from the coffee cup and then held it close to her chest for a few moments as she stared at me. Appraising me. She took another tentative sip. "Have you heard of the shift that's happening in the Universe?" she leaned in close and whispered.

Without realizing it, I had also leaned in to her. I straightened up and stretched my neck from side to side. I scratched the space above my lip and rolled my shoulders.

"You mean the environment?" I asked, not quite sure what she meant.

7

She nodded. "Sure, that's part of it. The environment is just a symptom of a greater shift that we're heading towards. The whole world is on the eve of a new consciousness, a new power and a new realization of the resources within the self. What is happening in the world is merely a wake-up call for the new consciousness. Have you heard of the precession of the equinox?"

I shook my head. I regretted asking. I had heard of all sorts of doomsday prophecies before. It reminded me of the Y2K pandemonium or the Hale-Bopp comet or the Waco Texas massacre. It seemed there was always a new end of the world theory. I wasn't very interested, but it was too late to get out of the conversation now. I was the one who'd asked.

Natalie twirled one finger around a dark tendril of hair. There was a glimmer in her eye, a little mischief hidden behind the smile she was trying to hide. Her gaze locked onto mine, and I could see miniscule orbs of light dancing in the greens of her irises. I looked away.

Natalie continued, "The shift that's occurring is going to change everything, I mean, life as we know it. It's been foretold by all the great mystery schools, and now we see the manifestations of the old prophecies. All the ancient secrets are coming true. It's exactly like they said would happen. The shift is happening just like they predicted." She paused, gauging my interest before continuing to explain. "You see, the earth spins in cycles, cycles of the earth's axis and cycles of constellations, and when the shift happens, civilization changes. Consciousness changes. What we know changes. How we communicate changes. Our awareness changes."

"And that's happening now?" I asked, going along for the ride.

"Yeah, look around, Selena. It's occurring all around us. They say it's going to start with a time of unprecedented disaster, natural catastrophes, war, violence, collapse of the old systems, destruction of the earth. Look what's happening around the world. After the shift happens, there will be a new reality and a new world unity."

"So what are you re-, I mean, what are you searching for in Jerusalem?"

Her expression changed, dimming the light dancing in her eyes. She lowered her eyelids and shook her head, making her earrings swing like pendulums against her smooth cheeks.

"It might be better for you not to know."

"What do you mean?" I asked, suddenly curious.

She smiled at me, biting her lower lip as she did. "It's not something that you can just hear casually. I mean, it's not something that you can just ignore, once you know."

"Know what?" I asked, squinting at her because I was confused.

"Do you really want to know? Because, once you know, you can't just pretend you don't. Once you know, some pretty weird things start to happen, and you can't just pretend you don't see them happening. You can't just go on with your day-to-day life and expect everything to remain the same. Once you know, changes start. So maybe it's better not to know at all. Not unless you're ready."

Now I was *really* curious. I thought about my life. School. Work. Repeat. I didn't really mind if my day-to-day life didn't remain the same. I didn't really believe that it could change that much.

"Sure, I'm ready," I assured her.

"Okay, don't say I didn't warn you." She beamed like the Cheshire cat. "They say there is a woman called La Que Saba..."

My quizzical expression must have revealed that I didn't know what that meant so she lowered her voice to a whisper. "It means One Who Knows. She's a Story Woman, a Prophetess. Like the Oracles from the old mythology. She's called the Nevea. They say she has come to reveal the secrets of the sages, to give the keys to ancient wisdom. I've heard that she has come to teach and prepare whoever is ready for the truth. I'm going to try to find her. There are a whole bunch of us going to look for her. Light Workers from all over the world are coming."

"And you're all meeting in Jerusalem?"

"Well, sort of. Communicating with each other has been really difficult. We started a few discussion groups on the Internet, but every time we try to make plans, we get closed down. So we started making our exchanges covert. We call ourselves peace activists, and we started an organization called Conduits of Consciousness, but we're really searching for the Nevea. See, the government knows all about her and wants to make sure that no one finds her. They're doing everything in their power to make sure we don't meet."

In that moment, I was sure that all of my suspicions about her were correct. She was just another conspiracy theorist thinking everyone was out to get her, that even the government was in on it. There really were crazy people everywhere in the world, and I really didn't have the interest or the inclination to go there. Call it curiosity but I decided to keep playing with her.

"Then how will you know where to look for her?" I asked, not even being careful to hide the skepticism from my voice.

Natalie either didn't notice or ignored my tone. "We'll follow the signs," she answered.

"What does that mean?" I stood against the galley wall, one foot perched behind me.

"Well, as Carl Jung called them—synchronicities. You see, there's no such thing as coincidence. Anything that has meaning to you is a sign that you should follow it. It's the Universal Mind speaking to your subconscious. The moment you bring your attention to these signs, they start to appear in your life to lead you. It's like the cosmos is guiding you."

I gave a skeptic smirk. It all sounded too 'woo-woo' for me. Ancient secrets, cosmic signs and shifts of consciousness were the fanciful dreams of metaphysical morons. I had met a lot of these kinds of new age zombies, stoned out of their minds, at college parties. Those people who believed the world was doomed unless they all started to chant like hypnotized hippies. I kept my smile hidden from Natalie. I didn't fall into the alternative culture. I didn't meditate, didn't eat granola, didn't even own a pair of Birkenstocks. I was proudly pragmatic, dependable and reasonable. I didn't have time. I had tuition and rent to pay, textbooks to read, teeth to floss.

Little did I know that my world was about to change.

Natalie handed me her empty coffee cup with a little shrug and stepped into the lavatory. I took the opportunity to sit down in my jump seat. Maybe if she saw me engrossed in reading, she would get the hint that I wasn't interested. I opened my book to the first chapter and began to read.

> *History is not what happened, but what has been recorded.*
>
> *It is said by linguists that language is changed by armies; that is also true for the ancient folklore, as it suffers adulteration by the conquerors to any region.*
>
> *A better understanding of history is achieved when we study not what has been written, but what has been omitted.*
>
> *We must shine a light into the corners of antiquity to reveal the secrets hiding there. The difficulty is that there are no corners in a round room.*
>
> *The past two millennia of conventional historical texts have pointed to a richly entrenched patriarchal society.*
>
> *His-story.*
>
> *The story told by the conquerors, in order to suppress the voices of the conquered.*
>
> *The story told by men, in order to suppress the voices of women.*
>
> *All reference to the society that saw the birth of the common history of Western civilization has been systematically and often violently restricted.*
>
> *But, society did not begin in patriarchy.*
>
> *Beginning in the Ice Age as the Earth Mother and well into the Neolithic Age, as agriculture*

became the predominant means of survival, Goddess culture flowered.

The Goddess religion was earth-centered, holistic, intuitive and accessible. The Goddess was the life force, within a larger web of the greater life force. All that lived encompassed the sacred fabric. Each person was part of the greater whole. Humankind, women equally with men, animals, plants, rocks, rivers, the planet and the atmosphere were all responsible for the rhythms of life.

The paradigm shift from Goddess to God, from a matrilineal society to a patriarchal one, from a worldly reverence to an other-worldly one, from a sensual practice to an ascetic one, deeply affected every human relationship. The balance of nature, equality and regeneration of life was knocked off kilter.

The demise of the Goddess has led to the brink of planetary annihilation.

In reclaiming the Goddess, we can correct this imbalance.

We can recover our true knowledge. We can live in harmony with our natural environment. We can learn new patterns of behavior. We can live in peace, harmony and gentle co-existence.

"When are you going to Jerusalem?" Natalie interrupted my reading, stepping out from the lavatory. I guess the hint didn't work.

"Oh, I'm not. I'm just staying in Tel Aviv."

"That's a shame to come all the way here and not go see the Old City."

I got up from my jump seat to face her eye to eye, sliding my book into the folding pocket in front of me. We were the same height, I realized, taller than the average woman. Her gaze was once again hypnotic; she seemed to look into my eyes and beyond. It was unnerving. I moved toward the galley counter and started to tidy up, wiping the ledge, stowing the equipment, trying to appear busy.

"I'd love to see Jerusalem one day, but I don't think now is a good time. Everyone says it's too dangerous," I answered as I used a paper galley towel to wipe down the oven doors.

In the three months I had spent working for the airline, I had travelled to some of the cities I had always dreamed of: London, Paris, Amsterdam, Tokyo. The layovers were always short, but I managed to get just enough time to make a whirlwind tour of each city. But that was before I went back to school. Now I had essays to finish and studying to do, the weight of my tuition grounding me. And the beach in Tel Aviv seemed like an ideal layover hangout.

Besides, I liked the solitude that came with traveling solo. I liked being a homeless soul, vagrant and ungrounded. I felt that I was in constant search of the great unknown. Not a solitude that can be quantified. Not a reclusive hermitage into an obscure cave. But, like the rest of my life, it was a solitude amongst and around people. It was a solitude that constantly reminded me how helpless I was. A solitude that made me realize I was weightless and unencumbered. Anonymous among many, I could disconnect from my loneliness.

When I'd told my roommate Beth that I was thinking of going to Jerusalem, she adamantly warned me against it. My teachers implored me not to go and the media seemed to confirm their fears daily. Despite all the warnings and admonitions, despite the chaos and the mayhem, despite my own better judgement, I felt a strong desire to go.

Natalie laughed, making her earrings dangle and her bracelets jingle. She looked at me with a mischievous grin. "Do you always do what people tell you?"

"N-No, I guess not," I stammered, embarrassed.

"If you would love to do something, then being warned of the danger is your first clue that you should do it." She smirked, with her lips pursed in a half-smile. "Don't people always warn you of the dangers of flying?"

"Yeah, I guess they do." I laughed, thinking of how many times I'd explained to people that flying is safer than driving, sometimes safer than walking. Everyone, including me, was surprised when I decided to continue flying after what was supposed to be just a summer job. I didn't want to give it up. For me, every flight was magical. I loved looking out the windows and seeing us sailing in a sea of clouds. I loved the miracle of being in the air. I also loved exploring every crevice, corner and character of the world. That's why the decision to leave the job was such a hard one to make.

"Do you think it's safe to go to Jerusalem right now?" I asked.

Natalie pushed her shoulders back and stood straighter. "Don't live by fear. That's what society would have you do. Live your potential. Anything less is like sleepwalking through life. Come to Jerusalem and help me find the Nevea," she said, with a coy and beguiling smile.

"Even if I wanted to go to Jerusalem, shouldn't I go on a guided tour? Won't that be better for my first time?"

"A guided tour will never bring you to the place you're searching for."

I narrowed my eyes at her, uncomfortable with her assessment of me. "What do you mean? I'm not searching for anything."

"You don't want to meet La Que Saba?"

I shrugged. "Well…sure…that would be great. But I just don't see how likely that is, to just walk into Jerusalem and…"

"It's not very likely to happen if you're not searching, but once you are, the path opens to you."

"Still, I just don't see how…"

"If you had the chance to meet the oracle, La Que Saba," she asked, with a sweep of her bangled arm, "someone who could answer any question you ask her, wouldn't you want the opportunity to ask?"

I wasn't expecting her question, and for a moment, I was speechless. I stumbled on my response, though I knew her question was rhetorical. There was, in fact, one thing I would love to know. It was the one question I'd never had the nerve to ask my mom because I'd never wanted to hurt her. It was the one thing I would do over, work up the courage to ask her, if she were still alive. It was the one mystery that burned into my psyche and that kept me awake at night. The one thing that awoke my loneliness every time I tried to forget about it. Yes, there was one question I would ask. But, even an oracle probably wouldn't have the answer. And I would probably never know the truth.

"Then think of it as a field assignment," Natalie offered, switching tactics. "The great anthropological field study, conducted by none other than Selena Silver. It could even be your thesis paper. You would probably get published, get a teaching offer, tenured, the works."

I considered what Natalie had said. Finding this Nevea, this La Que Saba, as she called her, would make a great topic for my assignment. Then I could actually justify going to Jerusalem instead of doing my research by reading a book on a Tel Aviv beach. It could be like an anthropological experiment. It was an investment in my future. It was a break from the ennui of studying boring textbooks. I shrugged my shoulders and smirked.

"Good. Then you can come to Jerusalem," Natalie said with finality.

I couldn't tell if she was inviting me or challenging me.

"Remember, follow your signs and trust your intuition," Natalie said as she turned to face the aisle, heading back to her seat. "See you in Jerusalem."

It wasn't until the end of the flight, once all the passengers had deplaned, that I took the book out of my jump seat and put it into my flight satchel. It was then that I happened to see the picture on the back cover. My breath stopped. My whole body got tingles. I stared at the title on the cover, and noticed for the first time: *The Return of the Goddess,* by Natalie Rose.

CHAPTER 2

Wednesday, September 28ᵗʰ, 2000
The Office of the Prime Minister, Jerusalem

The Prime Minister sat back in his chair behind the cedar-wood desk and pressed his fingertips together. In front of him stood a panel of his most dedicated and loyal strategists, some members of the legislative body, men and women in his majority left-wing alliance, as well as the ministers of the opposition party. The air was stiff with the implication of the opposition's request. Each member of the legislature drew their own opinion, but none were willing to intervene in such a potentially explosive matter. They were used to political flare-ups, but this was a matter beyond their experience. The windowed wall behind the Prime Minister's desk overlooked the Jerusalem hills, drawing the eyes of the cabinet members away from the unsettling ambience in the office.

"And you really think this is a wise move? Have you even considered the ramifications? Is it worth the risk?" He directed the questions at his right-wing political rival, but it was the Internal Security Minister who answered instead.

"I have received every assurance from their Security Chief that as long as we don't enter the mosque, there will be no issues." The Internal Security Minister stepped forward slightly, recalling the phone conversation he'd had with the Security Chief of the Palestinian authority. The two men, both in charge of security for their respective factions, had always had curt but courteous communications. The response, however, had been overly accommodating and suspiciously timely. But the Internal Security Minister did not divulge that information.

"Still, I cannot in good faith warrant that to be true. The public perception alone would dismantle the peace process. I will not consent to it." The Prime Minister stared at his opponent.

The sands of time had worn on them both, but the opposition leader had aged far beyond his years. It was a political reversal of power. The Prime Minister had once been a young cadet, serving under the Old Soldier when he had been a cutthroat military general. Even as a relatively young man, the General had earned the moniker Old Soldier, partly because he had been responsible for some of the most successful military skirmishes and legendary battles, but also because his tactics were considered by many to be archaically aggressive. The irony of the situation was not lost on either man. The dovish Prime Minister, who used to take orders from the hawkish Old Soldier, now sat in the highest possible government seat. The tables had turned. The dove had risen above the hawk, the tail of the lion dominating the lion. Like Einstein's parable of the lion's tail being proof that the lion exists, the Old Soldier adamantly refused to release his hold of the lion's tail, even though the popular vote had elected the peaceful policies of the current administration.

It was almost more than the Old Soldier could take. He had been a decorated soldier, strategic commander, and national hero. His many years in the army had made him militant, rigid in both his position and ideologies. But the years since his retirement from the strict military regime had made him fat and haggard.

"You and I both know we cannot let them…" The Old Soldier paused, caught his breath and quickly glanced from the Prime Minister to the assemblage. "Can we speak privately?"

The Prime Minister nodded at the cabinet members and they quietly acquiesced. Once they were alone, the Old Soldier approached the desk, his rubber shoes squeaking on the polished Jerusalem stone tiles. He sat down heavily, his elbows resting on the gleaming tabletop, and leaned his head forward. With his hands in front of him, he gestured in swift, assertive movements.

"My friend, my brother, I have spoken with the archaeologists in the tunnels. They feel they are very close. They're sure there is something of extreme significance under the grounds. You and I both know we cannot let such a find get into the wrong hands. Those idiots are getting too close with their bulldozers digging on the grounds. We can't have another debacle of an excavation like they did the last time. Imagine what those imbeciles might have unearthed! And they had the gall to dispose of it like refuse! Like useless garbage! Antiquities! Thrown like trash! It is our luck that there were only simple artifacts in that pile. Imagine if they'd actually unearthed anything significant? We must send the message that tampering with historical evidence will not be tolerated!" Spittle sprayed out of his mouth as he spoke.

"The message it will send will be one of hostility," the Prime Minister answered calmly.

"Listen," the Old Soldier said and pointed his finger antagonistically. "You know what the latest translations of the scrolls have indicated? What do you think that means? The archaeologists have assured me that the implication of a further discovery is imminent. We need the location to remain *in situ*, untouched. We need time. We need a distraction! The guards will be so busy with my presence on the grounds that it will buy our experts just enough time to go underground."

"We cannot take the risk."

"We can't risk NOT taking the risk!" The Old Soldier roared back.

The two men glared at each other for a few contentious moments while the Prime Minister considered the proposition. He knew this move would revive his popularity at the polls and restore the people's confidence in his left-wing policies by revealing the arrogance of the Old Soldier's right-wing fundamentalism. The international community would surely see it as a provocation by his opposition, an attempt to sully the peace process. And he would be safe as long as he could remain above suspicion and make sure no association between himself and the Old Soldier was leaked to the media. The Old Soldier would be deemed a renegade, anti-diplomatic, a dead weight to the current political climate. Finally, the Prime Minister envisaged, he would have the people's full confidence.

The Prime Minister broke the silence. Calmly, he tried another angle. "It is not an opportune time. The peace-niks have renewed their initiatives. They have become more vigilant, more active."

"Ach, when are they not active?"

"Yes, but this is different. They are becoming more organized, consolidating their efforts. They are uniting and communicating with each other. It doesn't help that they're speaking of the woman legend again."

The Prime Minister picked up his pen and twirled it between his fingers, an action he made whenever he was nervous. He caught the Old Soldier's gaze and put the pen down, but it was too late. Both men knew who was winning the argument.

The Old Soldier leaned back in his chair and crossed his arms over his massive midsection, lacing his fingers together to make the link. "So what? So, we have more *meshuganes*, more crazies, running around Jerusalem. As if we don't have enough of our own." The two men smiled, slightly easing the tension between them.

"I promise you," the Old Soldier softened his tone. "I beseech you. I ask of you, give me thirty minutes. It is just long enough to create the distraction we need. Give the archaeologists thirty minutes to get their men into the Well of Souls. Let them get whatever is in the cave. Let us rest assured that the treasure gets into the right hands."

"And what if our men don't find anything?"

"If our men can't find it, then neither will theirs."

The Prime Minister picked up the pen again, then realized he was doing it mid-twirl, and put it down. He placed his two hands together as if in prayer and tapped his lips with his forefingers.

"What if you're wrong? How do we defend this to the international media?"

"Simple. We send the message that my visit is in retaliation to the illegal excavation they had the nerve to perform this summer. We let them know that the destruction of any archaeological findings will not be tolerated. That they cannot get away with destroying evidence, proof of our history. You know they'll erase every sign, remnant and memory that they find. We will send them the message that the *Waqf* does not have authority over antiquities!"

"It will cause an uproar," the Prime Minister reiterated.

"We have their Security Chief's assurance. I will not step one foot into a mosque. I will not say a word. I will look around and I will leave, just like a tourist."

The two men sat in silence for a long time. The Prime Minister swiveled in his chair and stared at the vista of the Jerusalem hills. The view was breathtaking, a constant reminder of where he now sat, which still surprised him whenever he contemplated it. He leaned back in his chair and closed his eyes. As he often did when he faced a dilemma, he silently asked his ancestors for direction. Equally as often, they sat silent on the matter.

"What is it that you need?" The words came out in whispered acquiescence.

"A hundred men. Maybe two."

The Prime Minister pressed his fingertips together and brought them to his chin.

"God help us if you're wrong," he said, from behind stiff lips. "God help us."

23

CHAPTER 3

Wednesday, September 28th
The Chairman's Compound, Ramallah, West Bank

The room was full of men, and though a few heads were left uncovered, most wore the trademark black and white *keffiyeh*, in homage to the Chairman. Many stood, though some of the older men sat in the plush armchairs and sofas, remnants from the Chairman's time in exile. The walls were adorned with gilded frames, containing oil-painted portraits of the region's rulers, men in military regalia, blatant expressions of power. On the floor of the large, circular room lay carpets of the finest threads—Persian, Turkish, Indonesian—a sea of colorful tapestry.

The Chairman leaned back in his chair and struggled to put his feet up on his mahogany desk. It would have been a fluid move for a man half his age, but the Chairman had lost his youthful agility in his advanced years. After great effort, he managed to land one of his boots heavily on the desktop. It remained there uncomfortably. All the men in the room recoiled at the insult, but they knew to whom it was directed. The message the boot implied, a grave offence to the men of this culture, didn't affect the Secretary-General. He'd been involved in diplomatic work for much too long to become ensconced in the power struggles of politicians.

The rest of the men stepped back, but the Secretary-General was not deterred. He stepped forward in tandem with his cane, a souvenir from his time in Lebanon, as was his prosthetic leg. A diminutive man, the Secretary-General was down to earth and an emerging charismatic leader of a moderate political faction. His dark, kind eyes obscured his unmitigated genius, though he was humbly unaware of it. He kept his head uncovered, looking more like a Western diplomat than a Middle East political pundit. His appearance matched his political leanings, and he did not keep secret his distaste for the corruption and human rights abuses of the current legislation. A staunch advocate for democracy, he vociferously condemned the previous elections, accusing the legislation of rigging them. He campaigned heavily for democratic reform, appealing for an international governing body to oversee the election process. The Secretary-General's proposed policies of reconciliation were not warmly embraced by the Chairman.

"It does not make any sense," the Secretary-General argued. "Why would they make such a request? Why would they take that chance? With the peace accords lagging, giving that Old Soldier permission to enter the grounds of *Haram al-Sharif* is a mistake. I think this request of theirs is a ruse, some sort of media opportunity. I think we should investigate the matter further before arbitrarily consenting."

"Ha! A ruse for what?" the Chairman barked back. "That old idiot is just trying to get the media's attention. That swine is so arrogant. He always has been, and he can't see past his nose.

That Old Soldier, he'll get what he deserves, bloody murderer. It is good. Let that rotten pig get the world involved. I want CNN there, the BBC, Al Jazeera, I want them all there. I want the world to see this. That fat soldier is going to be a good instigation for an *intifada*."

"And what of the peace process, Chairman? You yourself signed the agreement, remember? Are you prepared to abandon it entirely?" the Secretary-General asked sardonically.

The air in the room thickened. The Secretary-General was notorious for his candor, a quality that most endeared him to the people. It was also the trait that the foreign attachés most respected, which explained why many of the diplomats preferred to negotiate with him rather than with the Chairman's delegates. But, in this environment, that kind of forthrightness could be deadly.

"It is not in my hands." The Chairman raised his hands in mock innocence. "I will not do anything that will be deemed as retaliation, but I cannot help what the enraged people do." His mouth turned up in a crooked smile. "You know what they say about me; I never miss an opportunity to miss an opportunity."

The Chairman's aides chuckled. He again gave them his famous side-of-the-mouth grin. "Let the retaliation come from the civilians. They will not abide by this insult to the *Haram al-Sharif.* This is just the opportunity they've been waiting for."

"I do not agree, Chairman!"

All of the men froze. Few dared speak so bluntly to the Chairman; the ones who had were quickly imprisoned, exiled, or executed.

"I am the Chairman, not you!" the Chairman roared back.

With an angry wave of his hand, the Chairman dismissed the Secretary-General and called forward his senior media advisors. They needed to begin planning his response to the international media organizations.

CHAPTER 4

Wednesday evening, September 28th
Tel Aviv

As the crew van drove through the bustling streets of Tel Aviv, the late afternoon sun was beginning to set over the Mediterranean. Orange light, scattered from the golden orb, cast a strange quality over the city. It mingled with the buildings, danced off the windows and whirled and nestled over the sand. The light created bronzed silhouettes of the people walking on the boardwalk.

The rest of the crew had already taken the seats at the back of the van by the time I got on so the only seat that was left was up front, close to the driver. I picked up Natalie's book from where I had left off.

> *For millennia, men have fought wars, but this does not mean that men are inevitably violent and warlike. Obviously, there were men and women in the prehistoric societies, when the power rested in a giving and nurturing ideal.*
>
> *Historically, all societies have been patterned on either a hierarchical/patriarchal model, whereby*

force or threat of force is inherently necessary, or a cooperative/matriarchal model, where force or violence is rendered unnecessary.

In the patriarchal paradigm, the dominance becomes stratified, in which a male-centric God dominates over male-centric angels, saints, then man who dominates over woman, child, animal and earth. The dominance of man is further stratified by heads of religions, heads of state and heads of man; all competitive and led by external rule.

Conversely, in the matriarchal paradigm, there is no dominion or power-over. Power exists from within the group. This creates shared leadership, with a cooperative or inner authority.

The van stopped and started, weaving through the traffic, daring to drive uncomfortably close to buildings, cars and pedestrians. In spite of my apprehension at the maniacal driving, or maybe because of it, I closed my eyes and let my mind wander. "Trust your intuition; follow your signs," Natalie had said. I tried to make sense of that cryptic sentence. For me, intuition was nothing more than instinct, an automatic response. I didn't believe that a person could know what was happening when they weren't there. I didn't believe it existed. I had never experienced it.

Except…there was one mysterious instance I could never explain. Just a few weeks after my mom had died, I was cleaning out her apartment. I had already moved my minimal belongings into student housing, donated her meager furnishings and scrubbed the small kitchen. I'd saved her bedroom for last. I was sorting through her papers, packing her clothes, and boxing her books when I had the strange sudden compulsion to sit down and read one of them. It was an old tattered copy of *The Prophet*, the spine fraying and the pages yellowed. It was a memento from the days she'd spent in the Peace Corps. I sat on top of one of the crates and read.

The words traveled through me like cascading waterfalls. I was lost in the beauty and poetry of the prose for hours. And then, with no explicable reason, I suddenly had the thought to look carefully at the back cover of the book. As my finger traced the seam, I felt an unusual thickness. With a small knife, I pried the last page from the binding. And there, to my surprise, was a thin stash of letters and a picture. I looked at the photo, an old sepia type, taken of my mother as a young woman, a long-haired hippy, sitting beside a dark-haired young man. She was smiling, facing the camera, while his gaze was only on her. His eyes were dark, rimmed with long lashes, and kind. Their hands were intertwined casually; their heads, tilted towards each other. Could that be my father?

I opened my eyes.

The van lurched and sped, screeching to stop for a red light. From outside the bus, I heard the flute like cry of a bird—*bly, bly, bly.* I looked around to see where it was coming from. Beside the bus was a low fence, on the top of which sat a bird, unblinkingly staring at me. Its little black head gave way to a body of gray feathers, but underneath its tail feathers, almost hidden behind its feet, was a shock of bright yellow.

I retrieved my notebook from my bag, flipping past the pages where I had glued the sepia picture and letters. I turned to a fresh page and began to draw. The driver looked in the rear-view mirror and noticed me sketching the little bird.

"You know about this bird?" he asked in heavily accented English.

I shook my head, but my eyes remained on the bird.

"It is Parsi story. You know what is Parsi?"

"Persian? You mean Iran?"

"Yes, yes. Old, old Per-jhun story." The light turned green, and the driver wrenched the bus into gear and continued, "This bird, bulbul, loved the white rose. So, God gave white rose name 'Queen of Flowers.' This bulbul was so happy that he wanted to dance with white rose, but he was cut by her..." The driver gestured with his hand as he searched for the word.

"Thorns?" I contributed.

"Yes, torns. The torns cut the bulbul and the blood of the bulbul made the white rose into red rose. You see, even in love, sometime we bleed."

"Very true." I nodded as I scribbled down the story.

"You stay in Tel Aviv whole time?"

"I haven't decided what I'm doing yet. Do you think it is a safe time to go to Jerusalem?"

"Safe? Of course it safe! It is holy city! Safest place in all world. You want Jerusalem, you tell me. I drive you. I give you good tour. Good price. We go tomorrow."

I pretended to contemplate the offer.

"Well? Yes? I take you?" he asked insistently.

"No. Thank you, but no."

"You go with tour bus? It no good. Too much people. I take you."

"I was actually thinking I should go by myself, just to explore."

He eyed me in the rear-view mirror. "No, that not safe." He shook his head.

"What? You just said Jerusalem is the safest place in the world."

"Yes, for mans, it is. For womans, no."

I tried to quell my fury, and I restrained myself from yelling at him. How dare he assume that just because I was female, I couldn't handle going to Jerusalem! I had been taking care of myself, without a man there taking care of me, since the day I was born, thank you very much! And, if he thought I couldn't handle exploring a city without being chaperoned like some helpless, little damsel in distress, then he had obviously never met me! Why did men always think they knew what was better for me? My resolve to go to Jerusalem strengthened.

"No, I think I'll go by myself," I snapped as assertively as possible.

"Okay, okay." He paused. "You know, many womans, they go to Jerusalem. They all are looking for the same thing. Womans! They look for shadows; they look for trouble."

It took me a few beats to register what he said. Maybe this driver knew something about La Que Saba after all. In a moment, all my anger abated. I felt a twinge of regret for so quickly sweeping away his offer to take me on a private tour.

In a hushed tone, I asked, "Have you heard anything about someone called La Que Saba? The Nevea?"

The driver eyed me in the mirror. "Oh, many, many years I have not heard this. It is nothing. A story from old womans. A mitt."

"A myth? You mean an old wives' tale? Like a legend?"

"Yes, yes, this is how you call it, a lej-hend. A story my mot-her learned from her mot-her, who learned from her mot-her." He waved his hand backwards denoting the antiquity of the tale.

"Can you tell me this legend?"

He raised his eyebrows. "You like stories, ahh?"

"I collect them." I surprised myself with my answer, as my pen hovered over a fresh page in my notebook.

"Okay, I tell you," he spoke as he drove, sometimes holding the wheel, sometimes not. "The women, they say there is a *payaam-bar*, a messen-jher between the Earth and the sky. This *payaam-bar*, they say she is a large bird called Simorgh. She has job to protect en-shent Per-jhun mystery. She is so old that she has looked at the end of the world three times. She lived so long, learned so much, that she has all the wisdom of all the ages. The womens say she is a *payaam-bar*, a messenj-er between earth and sky. She lives high, on the mountain, inside of the Tree of Life. The old womens would tell the lej-hend that one day the Simorgh would return, and they wait for signs. So the womens say to other womens, mother, she say to daughter, to say to her daughter, to look for signs. When that will happen, it will bring the Simorgh back. Then the Simorgh will show us en-shent mystery." The driver slowed for a red light.

"What is the ancient mystery?" I wondered out loud.

"Ahh, how can I know? I say to you, it is old womans story. How do I know what old womans tell?" He waved off my question with one hand.

We stopped. To the left of the bus was the aged, brick façade of the outside perimeter of some building. Again, I saw the strange, small bird sitting atop the wall. Again, it seemed to be staring at me.

"What is this on our left?" I asked the driver.

"It is old mosque."

I looked up and noticed the rooftop of a small mosque, its minaret looming. Spray-painted on the side of the wall was some graffiti with the letters angled upwards and the paint rolling down the edges of each letter. In black spray were the words *Know Peace.*

I smiled to myself, wondering playfully if that was my sign. Closing my eyes, I mulled the words over in my mind. I pronounced each syllable and rolled each letter around my tongue. In silence, I repeated the words: know peace, no peace, no peace, know peace. The words became a jumble of sounds. When I tried to make sense of them again, to iron them out so that they would once again lie flat as words, the thought struck me—there will be *No* Peace until we *Know* Peace.

I pictured that graffiti artist, creeping to the shadows of the wall in the night. Dressed in a black hooded sweatshirt, he produced the can of spray from the confines of his front pocket, deftly spraying the nine letters, before returning the can into the pocket of his hoodie and continuing into obscurity. I imagined his desire, courage and hope that this single act of civil disobedience might make a difference in the world. I also imagined his fear of being caught, overcome by the rush of excitement as his statement left its mark on the bricks: This was his solitary, defiant act of moral courage.

As the van made its final turn into the hotel, a small dot of yellow caught my eye. I turned my head to see the silhouette of the bird again. From the gateway of the hotel, the *bulbul* stared at me, barely visible in contrast to the glow of the setting sun. I knew in that moment, silly as it might sound, that my intuition had led me to my sign. I would not let fear, especially other people's fears, dictate my desires. I resolved that the next morning I would go to Jerusalem. I would guide myself by my intuition and look for the signs.

CHAPTER 5

Thursday night, September 29th
Old City of Jerusalem

I rubbed my eyes and adjusted to the light. The old woman followed me in and closed the door behind me. The glow from the lamp on the far side of the apartment cast a golden glimmer on her. Her aged silhouette was hunched, hinting at her years, and she wore a white tunic, with her gray hair knotted loosely at her nape. She looked kind and sweet, not at all like the gypsy lady I had imagined her to be.

I let my gaze drift around the luxurious room. Not large, but ornate, and one wall was completely covered in bookshelves, stacked haphazardly with gilded books. On the floor lay an oriental rug, its colors long since faded to a mottled amber hue. The walls, painted a deep mauve, were hung with gauzy linens and silky tapestries. It looked like a sultan's harem, rich and brocaded, out of place with the stone city that surrounded it. On the far wall was a window under which sat an antique looking divan. In the center of the room was a chaise lounge piled with cushions.

I had so many questions to ask her, but my mind was slow. My tongue peeled itself from inside the dry cave that was my mouth, and with heavy eyelids, I struggled to access my thoughts. I didn't really know how I had found her, or for that matter, if this old lady was the one who I was looking for, but I knew that I would rather be here than in the dark, winding streets outside. When would this chaos end? How would I make it out of the Old City? When would I leave? With dizzying confusion, I let the questions bounce in the fog of my mind.

Fuck, Selena, of all the stupid things you've done, this takes the cake, I silently berated myself.

I rubbed my temples and squeezed the inside of my eyes with thumb and forefinger. The past twenty-four hours seemed so unlikely, so surreal. The journey to find this old lady, to be in this Jerusalem apartment, was like a random series of events, perfectly orchestrated and perfectly mystifying. Like a cube with different colored squares, so infuriatingly puzzling, my mind could not quite piece it together.

We stood silently inside the entryway to the apartment for what became an uncomfortable pregnant pause. I was still hesitant to enter. From somewhere in the streets below, close by the sounds of it, I heard men's voices shouting angry and violent chants.

"You are like a fragile little bird with a broken wing. You resist the very help that will aid your healing."

I laughed nervously as gunshots rang out in the streets, much too close for comfort. Stepping inside, I felt groggy and disoriented. There was a familiar scent coming from the smell of baking bread and something garlicky-sweet. On the table sat a steaming teapot with two full glasses. My mouth was parched and the room beckoned.

"I don't really know what it is I should be searching for," I answered.

"Because you are searching, your path is changing." She invited me in with a sweep of her wrinkled arm, closing the door behind me. Sauntering to the divan, she sat down majestically. The movement was more like a dance than an action, more fluid than function. Every move she made was gentle and graceful, like an aged ballerina, swift and soft.

"You'll be safe here, little bird," she tried to assuage my fear.

I wasn't assured. I came to the edge of the chaise longue and sat down cautiously. The cushions were overly yielding, and like a child, I fell into them. Letting myself absorb the heaviness of the day, fear crept over me and a needle of panic stung me. I tried to recall what time I needed to return. The crew expected me back for pick-up on Friday evening. When had I left the hotel in Tel Aviv? Was it really only this morning? It seemed unlikely because so much had happened. The bus, the market, the tourists, the riots, the soldiers—it all seemed so long ago.

"Thank you so much for letting me in. I really appreciate it…I didn't really know where to go," I said as I struggled to sit upright in the overstuffed sofa.

The old woman's brown eyes twinkled in the light, the creases on the sides like well-worn river beds. She handed me one of the tea glasses from the brass table and picked up the other for herself.

She must have been an extraordinarily beautiful woman in her younger years. Her high forehead had an air of regality and her cheekbones were like small sweet plums, rising to meet her eyes every time she smiled. She had the wide and welcoming smile of a woman in her youth.

She shook her head. "No, no, just the opposite. I was expecting you. It is my honor for the grace of your visit. Besides, it's not safe yet. We will receive the sign when it is safe to go." She sipped from her teacup before continuing. "I was once a scared little bird myself. But that was before I learned to fly. I had only wings but not the knowledge to use them. Shame really, don't you think? Having such a gift and not knowing how to use it?"

"Like that story of the boy who had wings from mythology." I nervously laughed.

"Yes, just as in the story of Icarus." She gazed up, as if enjoying some distant memory. "I would love to hear you tell me this story." She leaned forward, balancing her teacup.

The sound of a helicopter hovering above interrupted us, and the crack of a gunshot pierced the air. It took me a few startled minutes to begin breathing again—until the whirring of the helicopter blades seemed to get a little more distant. "Well," I tried to piece together what I remembered of the story from my Greek mythology class, "Icarus dreamt of flying, so he and his father created wings out of feathers and wax. Then Icarus climbed up to the top of a tower and jumped with his arms spread wide. He started soaring higher and higher until he got too close to the sun. The heat of the sun melted the wax and the feathers all came off. Then he plummeted into the sea and died." I bumbled through the ending. I had forgotten it was such a dismal story.

"Ah, the story is remembered, but the riddle is lost. Unfortunately, spiritual teachings often mask the essence of truth with mystical words. You see, Icarus was imprisoned in a tower with his father, Daedalus. The tower sat in the center of an intricate labyrinth, a maze that Daedalus had himself created, trapped by an irate and jealous king. The wings were the gift Daedalus created for Icarus to escape. Yet, Daedalus had given Icarus something much greater than flight," she explained and gave me a poignant look, with one brow raised and a long finger gently stroking the other brow. "He said to him 'Fly the middle way. Do not fly too high or the sun will melt the wax on your wings and you will fall. Do not fly too low, or the tides of the sea will catch you.' Then Daedalus gave his son Icarus the greatest gift of all; he taught him the secret of the middle way. All the laws are the same, inner laws and outer laws. The same principles drive everything in this world. But, Icarus could not resist the temptation to fly upwards, to risk the heat. Once he began to fly, he forgot his father's warning."

"So, defying his father is what ultimately killed him?" I tried to sound innocent, but the sarcasm bled through my smiling lips.

"Ahhh, your interpretation reveals much about you, but very little about the essence of the tale." The ingenuity of her smile made me regret my cynicism.

"So what is the essence of the tale?" I asked, acquiescingly.

The old woman adjusted her tunic about her knees, smoothing the fabric with delicate fingers. I noticed for the first time that her fingernails were painted a deep mauve, matching the embroidery on the lapel of the tunic. Her legs were crossed at the ankle and on her feet were slippers made of thousands of tiny, shiny beads. The startling design of the beads mesmerized me for a few moments, an intricate pattern converging and repeating, growing in ever widening circles that looked like an exotic flower. When I looked up again, I saw that she was contemplating me, which should have been unnerving, but it was intriguing instead. I let myself sink a little deeper in the sofa.

"Imagine a pendulum. If you pull it in one way, it will swing back just as far the other way. It will live in the state of two extremes, first one way and then the other. The forces pushing it cause it to stay out of balance. Just as a hungry person would eat until uncomfortably full, a starving person would eat until illness. The degree to which a person acts is the equal degree to their reaction. But, neither extreme can last. Harmony exists only in the middle; the place where there is no energy pushing in either direction. When you spend your energy trying to maintain the extremes, nothing can move forward. The more extreme you are, the less forward movement there is."

I thought of the labyrinth of the Jerusalem streets. How lost I got within those stone alleyways and how it seemed that with every turn, I was getting deeper and deeper into the maze of the market. I thought of the street vendors, with their bellows, and the narrow, densely-crowded corridors. I thought of those hours I hid terrified in the doorway, hearing the upheaval all around me, terrified, hoping no one would find me. What if I'd had wings? I wanted to get out of there so desperately that I probably wouldn't have listened to reason either.

"Maybe gifts should be given with the instructions manual," I defended.

The old woman's smile was enveloping, like a myriad of waterways, starting at her mouth and traveling to the inlets of her eyes. Smiling made the skin around her eyes crinkle like rivulets. As she tilted her graceful head back, her white hair fell to her shoulders, and she made a little chirping sound of delight.

"My little bird, it is an act of grace to receive as much as it is an act of grace to give." She looked at me over her tea. "You were given it; you merely did not accept it."

"You're telling me that there is a manual for life?" I asked cynically.

"Yes, my little bird, in many ways there is. But often the manual is ignored, tossed aside in an attempt to figure it out by yourself. Is that not what you do?"

I shrugged. "I guess I like to figure things out myself. Isn't that what life is about? Trial and error? Trying and failing, but still trying?"

"That all depends largely on the creation myth you choose to adopt," she answered.

She uncrossed her ankles and slipped out of her shoes before folding her legs underneath her and straightening her tunic once more. I was surprised at the flexibility, ease and effortlessness with which she moved for a woman of her age. Her hands rested calmly on her knees. Without noticing I was doing it, I found myself mimicking her movements, sitting cross-legged on the sofa with my hands on my knees.

In an uncertain tone, I asked, "What do you mean?"

"If you explore the perennial philosophies of life, you'll find that your view of cosmology has had a great impact on your life.

Your creation myth is the foundation stone by which all of your choices, relationships, health and physical well-being are based. The creation myth you choose determines whether you believe that the world is a hostile place or a safe place, a journey through suffering or a lesson in ascension. The messages you receive from your society and upbringing color your view of your world and facilitate every decision you make, every word you utter, every emotion you have. Your beliefs affect how you view yourself and your place in the cosmos. Which creation myth was handed down to you, little bird?"

"Oh, I hadn't really thought about it," I stammered, blinking. "Is there more than one?"

She laughed softly. "There are three creation myths, and every culture in the world has subscribed to them in one form or the other."

"What are these creation myths?"

"The first myth, the one that most religions have fallen prey to, is that life is a trial. This myth espouses the idea that life is a test or a challenge, that earth is a training ground for souls that have not reached perfection and that the purpose of your life is to perfect yourself. This implies that there is something inherently wrong with you, that you are inadequate, that you must seek redemption or fulfill a predestined amount of suffering. Inherent in this myth is the notion that if you redeem yourself in this life, you will be rewarded in the afterlife. Of course, it entails the idea of earth as a fallen place, and that heaven must be a far distant, intangible place, that humanity must be exiled from paradise until enough hard work, enough self-sacrifice can be earned to return into the folds of salvation."

As La Que Saba spoke, I felt a twinge of recognition to what she was saying. I always felt distain for the stern, judgmental, father-figure in the sky. It was a God who wagged his finger at humanity and deemed everything as either; good or bad, right or wrong, decent or indecent, moral or amoral. It placed the onus of blame on human shortcomings in the eyes of the divinity for every war, natural disaster or conflict that happened in the world. Thousands of years of religions that told us to be "good," or whatever version of good they preached at the time, made us untrusting of ourselves and of others. That the battle between righteousness and evil, in which the winner only gets rewarded in a future world, was creating a present day world that was heading towards self-made disaster.

The implication was that if anything good happens, it is because you were judged to be good, but if anything bad happens, it is God's punishment or test. It was like a constant exam: love is conditional on being good and perfect. This view of life came with conditions—conforming to others' wills, to others' approval, to others' judgments.

"So, what is the second myth?" I asked, my eyebrows furrowing.

"Ahhh, that, my dear, is the myth proposed by the philosophers of modern age, during the time in history they erroneously named the Enlightenment. This myth suggests that life on earth is but a random accident, a chaotic series of events. Thus, humanity exists by a series of isolated incidents that happened to converge to create life. This view holds that the existence of other realms is unnecessary and mythical, that the spirit is imagined, that the world beyond our imperial senses is mere childish fantasy and superstition. Only the solid material, the stuff you can see and touch, and phenomenon are real. From this vantage point, it's easy to perceive that life begins sometime after conception and ends at physical death. There is no omnipotent judge, no afterlife, no unseen force. Other realms become the irrelevant and unnecessary teachings of the irrational, non-sensible belief systems."

"That doesn't seem like a myth at all! That sounds like common sense," I protested, sitting up straighter.

"The problem with this myth, little bird, is that it becomes internalized by humanity's view that life is an accident waiting to happen. It suggests that we can only control our lives by controlling the external circumstances. It forces humanity to safeguard themselves against all forms of threat, real or perceived. It creates a world where staying safe and secure is the priority. It promotes beliefs in lack, scarcity and competition. After all, if all that exists is the solid material that we see, then there's not enough for all, so people must protect what they have."

The old woman's hands had come up like flickering flames while she spoke. She returned them now to her knees, holding her thumb and middle finger together, in a pose that looked wise and all knowing. I thought back to Natalie's words. *They call her La Que Saba*, she had said, *the one who knows.* I looked at her again, this mysterious woman who was stimulating me to think about things in ways I had never considered before. Her eyes were closed in silent meditation. I copied her pose by closing my eyes and letting my mind wander.

I thought about what La Que Saba was saying. In my Western society, it seemed that everyone was so concerned with their own safety and survival that they closed themselves up into little boxes, installed alarms in their homes and on their cars, put secret codes onto everything they owned and fortified themselves against any potential threats. Yet, it also seemed that people were walking around in a constant state of anxiety. With all of their material possessions, their lives were lonely and empty. There were loads of books and self-proclaimed gurus out there teaching people about happiness and meaning and purpose, but the more we searched for it, the further away it all seemed to be.

"What, then, is the third myth?" I asked, surprising myself out of my inner reflections. I adjusted my legs and stretched them in front of me, trying to get the blood to flow again.

La Que Saba did not move at all. For a moment, I thought she had fallen asleep. Her eyes remained peacefully closed; her countenance, relaxed. After a few deep breaths, she spoke.

"The interpretation of the third myth is one that has been skewed and misconstrued since ancient times; yet, it remained alive and buried in the mystical teachings of all cultures. It sees human beings as part of the creation and creation as part of the whole. It sees desire and sensuality as part of the ever-evolving joy of creation, the purpose of creation as joy. It sees potential in the miraculous, unconditional love in the immanence of the soul. It is simply this: Life is a gift, and you are a gift to the world."

"Hmmm, that sounds more like it," I said as I relaxed my guard, allowing myself to sink back once again into the cushions of the chaise longue. "Why don't people know about this purpose of life?"

"Little bird, the purpose of life is the ubiquitous Holy Grail, the force that has made men mad and the question that has driven humanity to the depths of despair. Yet, the answers were always there, ready and available for all to behold. Encoded in the stories from every mystical tradition, the Seven Sacred Spheres were always present. Knowing them is the removal of the seven veils. They let you see all the colors of the rainbow, not as an arc, but as a full circle of luminous color. Thus you will unveil the aspects of yourself into the seven realms."

I narrowed my eyes, trying to follow what she was trying to explain. "What do you mean? What are these Sacred Spheres?"

"The cosmos are filled with infinite number of glittering spheres, each reflecting all the others, and therefore the reflections of the spheres in one another. Like the glittering spheres, in some way, every human being contains the reflection of everyone else. And if you look inside yourself, you will see that you *do* participate and react emotionally to what happens on your planet. Each person is the whole world."

"So, the Sacred Spheres are about the cosmos? Like a macrocosm? Or, like a microcosm?" I wished she would just speak in straight terms, rather than circling around everything like a riddle.

She smiled. "The microcosm *is* the macrocosm. The Spheres are qualities of human consciousness. These qualities are not abstract

47

concepts, but living beings. As living beings, it is possible to meet the qualities of consciousness, understand them, speak with them, spend time in their company. The Spheres can infuse you with their particular note, stimulate you, guide you, and inspire you."

I shook my head. "I don't really get it. What do you mean by qualities of human consciousness? Do you mean the idea of courage or happiness?"

"The spiritual concept of an idea is very different than being in contact with a Sphere. To experience a Sphere means entering a world of subtle perceptions and energy exchanges, but not as a mere concept, or an idea. Entering into contact with a quality of a Sphere can be every bit as real as the sensation of walking under the canopy of a softly swaying tree, or contemplating the ocean as you sit by the shore, or feeling the soft caress of a raindrop falling on your skin. These things cannot be explained. They must be experienced."

La Que Saba's eyes had remained closed as she spoke, at first calming me, but now unnerving me. She graciously opened them and smiled. She took a deep breath, and I found myself doing the same. I realized that I had been stretching forward in anticipation. I allowed myself to relax, bringing my shoulders down and unclenching my jaw. I even opened my mouth in a stretch and heard my jaw bones grind against each other.

"So, why have these Spheres been hidden? What's the secret?"

"If you uncover the secrets, reveal the codes, if you find them, then you find the purpose of every life and the purpose for humanity. *That* is the secret."

She was still sitting in her regal, cross-legged pose. The light in the apartment seemed to dim everywhere else except for on her, casting a glow that seemed like it was generated from within. She seemed younger somehow and I started questioning whether I had imagined her to be older than she was. She easily moved her legs out from underneath her, and resting them to her side, inclined towards the side of the divan, she brought one hand under her chin. In that very moment, her beauty was captivating.

"If they are secret then aren't they kept, well, secret?" Smirking, I peered closely at La Que Saba to see how she might respond.

She laughed softly. "Secrets are not created to be contained— that is the illusion of the secret. A secret is kept until its time has come to be revealed. Secrets expose themselves as answers, waiting patiently on the right questions. A thing like that is not written in any book. A thing like that is only written on the tongue, in the caress of a mother, in the florio of the hand, in the bounce and sway of the hip, and in the glimmer of an eye."

"So, how did they remain hidden? How did they not get lost?" I asked, as my legs tucked underneath me and my hand came under my chin, mimicking hers.

"There was a time, when the women would gather monthly, during the moon's cycle that mirrored the menses, a time of great magic and spiritual elevation. The women would leave the homes they shared with men and retreat into the place reserved for women, the Red Tent. That is when we would dance the secrets for each other, and sing of the secrets, and tell the tale of the secrets. And that is how the secrets were kept alive. The secrets have been hidden for millennia. It is time to reveal those secrets, to unwrap the gifts. The secrets have been waiting patiently for the time when they can reveal themselves. We, Story Women, must uncover the truth, disclose the secrets, dispel the illusion that has been kept throughout history."

"Why come out with this truth now? Why are these secrets ready to come out?" I tried to ask without sounding overly sceptical. I didn't think she noticed.

"Like an errant child who needed time to mature, the Earth went through a dark time, but the Story Women knew, even as the tides of time were replacing the secrets with stories of shame, guilt and fear. Stories of Hell and of suffering. Stories of darkness, chaos and despair. The Story Women saw this happening, so they wrote their secrets on parchment or painted them on walls or pottery. They hid them in scrolls and jars. Then they whispered the whereabouts to their children until they were ready to come to light."

"So where are these secrets? Who has them? Who knows them?"

"The ancient wisdom was spread by emissaries throughout the world, whispered through the generations, and hidden in scrolls. Now the signs that have been anticipated are presenting themselves."

"The signs are presenting themselves?" I asked, doubtfully. "Isn't it just that people have gotten better at finding them?"

"The truth often hides within open spaces, as the secret knows how to protect itself through the ignorance of others. Just as the secrets that came out of hiding for the young shepherd boy in the desert and the farmer in the caves. And there are more that are waiting to reveal themselves. More are being found even as we speak. The problem lies not in what the secrets reveal, but into whose hands they fall."

CHAPTER 6

Thursday night, September 29ᵗʰ
Old City of Jerusalem

There was a commotion in the alleyway outside of the apartment. I perched upright, immobilized in fear. Every fiber of my being was apprehensive, listening as the voices screamed at each other what I could only assume were words of anger and hatred. I looked at the old woman for reassurance. She seemed serene and calm, totally oblivious to the rebellion outside. As the voices tapered off, still shouting into the far off distance, the apartment returned to relative quiet, and I felt the muscles of my body slowly releasing their tension.

"Would you like to learn the secrets?" she asked once I had relaxed enough to listen.

"I guess so," I said, realizing that she was trying to distract me from the chaos. "What are these secrets?"

La Que Saba effortlessly got up from her seat and walked to the window behind her. I watched her every dance-like movement, awed by her grace and ease. Every move she made had an assured quality; her arms made grand sweeping motions as she pulled on the lever for the blinds. Everything about her was soft and feminine, reminding me of Natalie. With the blinds completely closed, the room felt safer, shielded from the outside world. She continued to stand while speaking again, her voice reverberating in the room with a little audial ricochet. The echo was comforting, lulling me into a state of calm once again.

"The Seven Sacred Spheres represent a spiritual journey that every human being must make. We are all given these assignments in life. Your purpose is to discover and unveil within yourself the hidden wisdom. This unveiling does not take place by means of concepts in a logical process, but by means of symbols and the fire they ignite within you. Symbols that you attract, activate and come to understand. That is the unification of the Creator within the Creation. Your purpose is for your life to be an expression of creation. Until it is expressed, it cannot be experienced. The first of all the Spheres is to Explore your Essence. As was inscribed on the Temple of the Oracle at Delphi—*Know Thyself.*"

I thought of the personality type assessments they used to give us in school, the ones that were supposed to show you your strengths by the type of answer you gave to any situation. Mine always came up as independent and logical. As if I didn't already know that.

"Do you mean strengths and weaknesses? Like, what career I should choose?"

She shook her head. "That is a product of the world you are living in. Most people today put more emphasis on the material aspect of their character, what they do, what they have, rather than who they are at their core. Essence is like water, a pure energy that when added to something else, brings that thing to life. Essence is your soul energy, so no matter what task or activity or career you choose, you bring it to life by bringing your essence to it."

I ran my hands through my hair, thoroughly confused. "What does that mean?"

"This means that every soul comes into this life to fulfill a certain mission, the soul's true calling. It does not matter which steps you take to reach that. It only matters that you explore what your individual essence is. That is the essence of your being, the luminous nature of your consciousness. It is the fundamental element in your soul's growth. If the essence of your soul is fulfilled, your soul can expand to reach higher forms of potential. If your soul's essence is ignored, then conflict is inevitable. Your essence is your soul's calling. It is what you know exists in your heart. Your essence is your gift to the world. Because there is only one you in this lifetime, and if you betray your essence, it will be lost to the world. You are the only channel to the creation of that essence." While talking, La Que Saba sat back down. Her hands, illustrating circles, came together over her heart and then opened towards me.

I watched her hands and leaned forward. "Isn't part of knowing my essence just a matter of knowing what I think about? The way I see things? The way I feel about them?"

She gently touched my arm. "Little bird, human life is merely a vacation for your spirit. Humanity allows you, the essence of you, to experience feelings, thoughts, sensations that you do not have in light form. Your soul longs to feel, to really experience, the full range of human emotions, human sensations, human desires. Everything that this life offers you, your essence wishes to experience."

"So, how do I find out what my essence is?"

"Your essence is not an activity, or something you do. It is your purpose for being. You can only come to know it by exploring your heart. It is the only way to live and experience inner peace and harmony. Exploring your essence is your process of individuation. It is the responsibility of your life, the development of self-realization. This is the necessary journey that every human must make, aligning the form that exists in this material reality with the potential that exists in the spiritual realm. The experience and acceptance of these two opposing forces contains the possibility of their integration, which would lead to a further development of consciousness."

I let myself sink comfortably into the sofa, my gaze drifting towards the expansive bookcase on the wall. I had always loved books. Since childhood, they had been my playmates, my refuge, and my friends. I often preferred the company of books to the company of people. So, despite being raised by a single mother, and moving so often that it was impossible to keep friends, as well as being painfully shy, I grew up in a world of fantasy where I had two loving parents, a plethora of relatives, and throngs of interesting friends. Reading allowed me to untether from my reality. Fueled by my love of literature and imagination, I grew up free on the inside.

I read to the sound of my mother's tears at night. I read to ward off my secret longings. I read to remember things that I had never lived and I read to forget the things I had. I read to love and desire and yearn and lust.

I read to dream that one day my life would be different.

"How do I know whether I have found it or not?" I asked, trying to decipher if my love of books had anything to do with my essence. After all, shouldn't my soul be calling me to do something bigger, more substantial, more meaningful than just simply reading?

"Once you find your essence, you cannot resist it. If you betray your essence, then you betray yourself and inner conflict is inevitable. This is what makes you come alive. This is your gift. Your life's purpose is to learn how to harness your gift into loving and positive actions."

"What if I never find it?" I asked, sipping from my tea. I was embarrassed to ask her if my love of books could be my essence. The only thing I could truly say I found irresistible were stories; yet, I felt that reading was my escape and not my mission in life. I doubted whether something so passive could be considered a worthwhile mission.

As if hearing my thoughts, the old woman answered, "Like an author who writes a story, you write your life by which thoughts you accept and which you reject. Your life is a story written by the silent author who dwells within you."

I cocked my head to the side. "So my essence is just about what I think?"

"If the thoughts you think are enlivened with essence. When you add essence to anything, you bring it to life. It's like adding water to a seed. The seed is whole and complete on its own, but once water is added to it, the water activates the life potential inside it."

Her words tumbled in my head as if going through the spin cycle. The way she spoke, with her ethereal accent and mysterious intonations, made her words both cryptic and inspiring. Never before had I spoken with someone as rich in nuance and depth as this woman. I felt the inclination to write everything she said into my journal. Yet, I knew the words would not shine any more light if I read them later.

"So my essence is waiting dormant?" I asked, suspecting, like some carnival fortune-teller, she would see through me and proclaim my love of literature. The skeptic within me didn't want to reveal it to her openly. A voice inside my head started elucidating all the reasons I would give when she announced that given my love of literature, I should be an author. I kept repeating the litany of excuses, not being able to tell stories, not having anything to say, and not being able to come up with anything interesting. What if I found out that I'm not actually very good at it?

I realized I had stopped breathing.

The Nevea responded to my internal inquiry. "The seed of your potential is planted within you. It is only once you explore your essence that the potential for growth is watered. It is only once you explore your essence and align it with your intentions that you can expand your awareness and unleash your potential." The old woman made small gestures with her hands, like a gardener who is lovingly tending to her plants.

I thought about the society that I was living in. It was true, other than the few choices of 'types' or 'genres' that existed, no one really put any emphasis on finding out who they really were. It seemed that everyone was comfortable being compartmentalized, labeled, put into a box, and inspected by experts. There was no place for exploration, only blanket diagnoses of likes and dislikes, haves and have-nots, good and bad. Most people related their being through the things they do: I am a student, I am a doctor, I am a mother. They defined themselves by the things they say or the things they have: I am poor, I am rich, I am pretty. But, the idea of exploring a mission that is at the core of the soul was not something people normally spoke about. People were much more comfortable zoning out and watching television. As for me, I was much too busy. If I were to explore my essence, it would have to be quick.

"What if I never find out what my essence is?"

"That is your choice for this life. The opportunity will come again." She could sense I wanted a more refined answer, so she continued. "It reminds me of the story about the two butterflies. One butterfly peeked out of the cocoon, saw the vastness of the outside world and became too scared to come out. Within a short time, that butterfly became suffocated by its own creation. The other butterfly looked out of the cocoon, saw the vastness of the outside world and also became too scared to come out, but soon found that the cocoon it had created was too constricting and it was forced to break free. Once it was released from bondage, it saw that the world was truly vast, but also beautiful and radiant. That butterfly chose to accept the challenge of its fears and learned to fly."

I shivered because her story stirred a memory from my childhood. I was young, maybe five or six, when I found a cocoon in the backyard. My mother told me not to disturb it, that it contained a butterfly being born. I spent days watching it, waiting. Until, finally, I started to sense movement. I could see the butterfly struggling against the cocoon, fighting from within to free itself. It seemed like it was in pain, frantically trying to break free. I reached out my hand, intending to just give the butterfly a little help, but the chrysalis disintegrated at my touch. I cried for days, refusing to tell my mother what I had done. In my mind, I had murdered a beautiful butterfly, killed it with my hands.

"What if someone, or something, never gets to reach their potential? What if, um, circumstances, prevent it?" I enquired.

"Every living being has a soul mission and a purpose in this life. The circumstances will always present themselves to the highest potential of that individual purpose. It is not for you to judge what that mission is, just to explore what our own is," the old woman continued. "To both the butterflies, the vastness of the outside world was overwhelming. They did not need to seek it, but it came to them. The same is with you, little bird. You cannot deny your essence any more than the butterfly can deny that it must grow into a butterfly."

"How do I begin to explore my essence? What do I need to do?"

"Within each moment of each day, within each decision or indecision, you affirm or deny the gift of your uniqueness through the way you live your life."

"So I can just make choices that create the life that I want?"

The old woman nodded sagely. "The essence of your soul is vast and expansive. Its deepest desire is to know and experience its greatest potential. It naturally creates and evolves." She lifted one long, graceful finger and pointed it at me. "You are an intentional creation. The very core of your being cannot be denied because it sends messages to your cells reminding you of your power and uniqueness."

"What about my desires? How about all the things I want to do?"

"Desire is life, life is change and change is progress. You are constantly evolving. Life is constantly expanding until consciousness is at one with creation."

"Are my desires not my essence then?" I thought of the burning desire I had felt the previous night at the beach with Shai, the walk back to my hotel, the goodbye. I quickly put it out of my head.

"Desire is fleeting. Your soul is ever evolving. The entire universe is caught up in an expanding consciousness, because it is the nature of the universe to seek to know itself," she answered cryptically.

"So, do I just create my desires?" I raised an eyebrow, trying to understand.

The concept intrigued me, but I couldn't figure out how something that I felt as an impulse could be something I created. I never considered that my wants and desires didn't just come to me instinctively, like a knee-jerk reaction to what went on around me.

She smiled. "The essence of creativity is the love of life, for a life filled with love compels you to live bigger, do something better, be more enlightened. You will never be completely happy unless you fulfill your destiny, unless you enlarge your vision of your life."

I sipped my tea. The nervous butterflies flapped their wings in my stomach. How odd it felt to be sitting inside this strange woman's apartment discussing the secrets of life and sipping tea, while outside a furious rebellion was in full swing. It seemed myopic and indulgent to be discussing my personal essence while the world outside rocked with such violence.

As if reading my thoughts once again, the old woman countered, "The pathway to enlightenment begins on the inside. The cosmos is merely a mirror to the individual consciousness. Do not expect planetary transformation until your personal transformation has been fulfilled."

I sat back on the chaise longue, this time allowing myself to sink into it fully. As the soft cushions enveloped my body, so did my mind envelop my thoughts. I saw my thoughts hover within and around my mind; yet, somehow I saw that it was not me thinking those thoughts. I became aware of myself becoming aware of my thoughts. I was no longer the owner of my thoughts but a mere witness to them. I was no longer the feeler of my feelings but a spectator of them, not the object of my desires but the observer of them.

What I was was both beyond and within me; bigger and weightless; outside of me and integrally within me. I sat in the wonderment of that realization for what may have been hours or perhaps moments. It was complex, yet so simple, and I was fully, completely, utterly free.

CHAPTER 7

Wednesday night, September 28th
Tel Aviv

I should have been tired, but I was too excited by the prospect of being close to the ocean, so I decided to go for a walk along the beach. The sound of the waves was accompanied by the steady hum of sea air. The sound reminded me of the radio in my mother's Chevy Malibu, with a dial that when turned to find channels would emit steady static. It was a muffled sound, a noise that was both nothing and everything. It was the same noise as could be somehow magically captured inside of a shell.

It sounds like the ocean, my mother had murmured as she held the big shell she'd brought back from some long forgotten vacation and unearthed it years later in the mess of boxes after yet another move. She held it against the side of my young face. I didn't know what the ocean sounded like, but I pressed my tiny fingers against the cool, hard shell and listened. What I'd heard was not the ocean, but some sort of rhythmic wind. A recorded message left by the previous tenant.

"Can you hear that?" she'd asked.

I nodded, not sure I'd heard anything, and peered inside. The interior of the shell was smooth and glistening, such a contrast from the rough texture on the outside. I put my finger inside, curious to explore it. Something slimy and wet like a slug used to live in there, my mother had explained, and I pulled my finger out. My mother had laughed.

It was just like my mother to wonder about those little things. I was always amazed how she could become so excited about a shell, or a rainbow, or finding a lucky penny. She was so childlike, much more than I was. Like role reversal, I played the mom; she played the kid. She had me when she was so young that we were practically sisters.

After volunteering with the Peace Corps, she had come back pregnant and alone. Her parents, though they didn't disown her outright, did not approve of her choice to keep me nor of her choice to live a migratory existence, and I saw little of them growing up. The man who impregnated her was a distant, long forgotten memory, never mentioned, rarely acknowledged. She told me little about her Peace Corps years, becoming quiet, hesitant and quickly changing the subject if I asked. Throughout my childhood, I never asked about him. Asking would mean she had failed me. Asking would say she wasn't enough. Asking would hurt her. So I never asked and she never told.

We lived amongst the things left unsaid that became part of the background. Tiptoeing around them, we carried them with us from one apartment to another. I got used to those things; they were my playmates, my imaginary friends. Not knowing who my father was let me create worlds in my fantasies. One time, my father was a foreign prince who would come and rescue me and my mother, apologizing for having abandoned us for so many years and whisking us away to his castle on his private island. Another time, I imagined that he was the kind, bearded vice-principal of my new school. Sometimes I would picture a man, and in my anger, I would imagine his regret and sorrow at having left us. In those moments, I would see myself turning away from him, hurting him with my rejection, like he had done to me.

As I grew older, and she got sicker, I was the one looking out for her, taking care of her. Every time we moved, I would pack the boxes and clean the apartment. Every time her heart would break from yet another disastrous relationship, I would pick up the shattered pieces. Now that she was gone, it was hard to adjust to life without her. I had no one to save. Now, whenever I thought of her, it reminded me of the pain, and she had become one of the things left unsaid.

The boardwalk was full of people. Couples pushing strollers were out for a late night promenade, old men sitting on low stools were playing backgammon, occasionally yelling at each other while spitting sunflower seed shells, vendors were selling cheap jewelry off makeshift tables, street buskers, pretending to be statues, stood on crates waiting for a few coins, while the waves crashed against the breakers. The sea air tickled my nostrils with every inhalation. It smelled like a bouquet of saline mist and vinegar chips.

One couple, walking hand-in-hand, could have been just like any other couple anywhere else in the world, except for the fact they were both dressed in soldier uniforms and had machine guns slung casually over their shoulders. I seemed to be the only one who noticed this as being an anomaly, because no one else even gave them a second glance as they passed.

Beachside restaurants lined the sandy shore, their sunken chairs facing the sea. I made my way down the steps. Closer to the water's edge, I was enraptured by the sound of the waves. The sheer volume was overwhelming. It completely drowned out the noise made by the families, old men, restaurants and vendors. From here, the ocean ruled out all other noise. Here, the ocean took control, rendering anything else inconsequential. Beside the vast ocean, I felt so small.

I stood transfixed, my breath matching the ebb and flow, as I watched the edge of the ocean playing tricks on my eyes as it stretched out as far as I could see. All beyond it was black. Limitless. Never-ending. Infinite. I remembered the stories of the first explorers, scared to venture into the seas, convinced they would fall off the edge of the earth. Standing by the edge of the vast ocean, I could understand them.

I rolled up my jeans, took my flip-flops off and walked on the sand to the water's edge. The crash of the waves was deafening. In the void, it boomed; yet, the water that rolled against the sand was soft and lulling. And then I heard another, almost imperceptible, noise from a distance. It sounded like the steady rhythm of an echoing pulse. I walked towards the noise, unsure of whether my ears were playing tricks on me or not.

As I walked, the throbbing beat got stronger. I passed the breakers and only then did the source of the noise come into view. There, in the darkness of the shore, removed from the lights of the city and beyond the length of the boardwalk, was a group of fifty or sixty people sitting in a semi-circle along the water line. Some had drums perched in between their legs or in their hands and some were hitting tambourines. In the center were a few poi dancers, balancing clear candles on their hands. Scattered between the drummers were tribal dancers, their bodies pulsating to the rhythm of the drums and the ocean. Graceful as acrobats, two men wearing white pants and bare torsos were engaged in what looked like a capoeira battle. Beyond the circle there were small groups of people relaxing in the sand, dancing with glow sticks laced between their fingers or juggling fire. There were a few girls tossing hula-hoops and some people were spinning devil sticks in the air.

The whole scene was phenomenal, like nothing I had ever seen before. It was far from a performance, although extremely enticing. The drummers, dancers and performers were not at all putting on a show, but were each, in their own way, simply celebrating. The fact that people were watching was neither an incentive nor a deterring factor: It was simply a part of the celebration. Every once in a while, someone from the crowd would get up and join in the dance, losing themselves in the ecstasy of the moment.

I found a place to sit, far from the crowd. The sand felt cool, smooth and mellifluous against my legs. I burrowed my toes into the sand and then raised them, watching the sand spill off my feet.

"*Yaffe, ah?*"

I didn't realize anyone was around me, but there he was, suddenly right beside me.

I tried to catch my breath because his voice had startled me, but looking at him didn't help. Even in the relative dark, I could feel that he was gorgeous. He was leaning back, elbows in the sand, bare feet crossed at the ankles. The light reflected his chiseled features, making me lose focus for a moment. His eyes met mine and held them far longer than I knew how to react to.

"Sorry, I don't speak Hebrew." I blushed, looking away and fiddling with the rolled-up cuff of my jeans.

"Oh, okay. English?" he asked, still looking straight at me. "Beautiful, isn't it?"

"Yes, yes, it is." I answered, grateful for the darkness that hid my timidity.

The waves slammed against the surf, creating a symphony of sound. A few gulls called into the night sky, adding their own version of musical effect. The drummers and dancers collaborated to keep the hypnotic rhythm, and I was mesmerized. I tried not to look at him, though his eyes were intensely staring into mine.

"Are you a tourist?" he asked, in his imperceptible accent. The intonation of the letter R, the emphasis on the end of the question, peppered his query with mystery.

I shook my head, still blushing. "No, actually, I'm here for work."

"Really? What do you do?" Once again ending the question with emphasis.

"I'm a flight attendant, here on layover. But, I'm also a student."

In a single gesture, he sat up, wiping the sand off his elbows.

"A flight attendant, ah? So, you have traveled around the world? Have you been everywhere?" His enthusiasm was contagious.

"I've been to a few places, yes." I worked up the nerve to meet his gaze, though only for a moment. But that was all it took. His deep eyes, cute dimples and beguiling gaze were so alluring. But, especially enticing was his smile. It was the most authentic and human testament of beauty I had ever encountered. It was the Adonis of smiles. Raw, intense and irresistible, it threatened to envelop me in its warmth. My whole body flushed.

"You are so lucky. I would love to travel around the world."

"Why don't you?"

"It's all in the plan." He gave me a flash of his stunning smile. "Once I finish my army service, I plan to travel for a year. Backpack through Asia maybe or South America. You know, the usual deal. But, to be able to do it as a job... wow, that is a dream."

I smiled. "Well, it's not all that. I can't pay for school unless I have a job, so..."

"You know what I think?" he interrupted. "I think you don't know how to enjoy yourself," he announced, his eyes searching mine.

The tempo of the surf, accompanied by the drummers, seemed to speed up, and it took me a few moments to get over the shock of his accusation. He said something else, and I couldn't tell if it was an introduction, or if he was making a statement. Above the crashing of the waves and the beating of the drums, I heard him say, or at least I thought he said—"I'm shy." I felt an overwhelming rush of emotion flood through me, because, even though I worked hard to conceal it, what I wanted to be able to say out loud is—"I'm shy, too!"

"It's my name, Shai." He smiled, a mocking gesture, surely meant to further embarrass me. "It means gift."

I blushed at my mistake. "My name's Selena. It means moon." I said, feeling like a dork the moment the words tumbled out.

"It's beautiful."

My blush intensified.

"Have you been to Israel before?"

"No, this is my first and probably last time."

"Why is that?"

"Well," I tried to find the simplest explanation, the one that would prove that, contrary to what he might have thought, I did know how to enjoy myself. "I started this job in the beginning of summer, thinking I would do it just until school started." I shrugged. "And now, I'm already a few weeks into school. I've been trying to do both, but I don't know if I can keep that up. I'm going to have to make the decision pretty soon, at least before I flunk out."

"Why don't you stay with the job? Take some time to travel and then worry about school later."

"It's complicated."

"It's only complicated if you make it complicated." His expression was smug.

"In my case, it really is complicated."

We sat facing the crowd of dancers, both of us with our elbows on our knees and our bare feet buried in the sand.

By his silence, I understood that he was still waiting for an explanation.

"My mom died in May." I waited for the usual dose of pity, waited to hear the requisite, *"I'm sorry,"* waited to answer the obligatory, *"It's okay. It's not your fault."* It didn't come. His expression hadn't changed. "Before she died, she asked that I finish school, get a career, pursue my passions. You know, not make the same mistakes she did."

"Was she sick for a long time?" he asked.

I nodded. "Years. Cancer."

"And your father?" he enquired.

"He left before I was born."

I looked out at the ocean and the vastness of it was incomprehensible.

"What are you studying?" he asked.

"Anthropology," I answered, grateful to be off the topic of my parents.

"Oh, yeah? That's interesting," he remarked, smirking at me.

"Why?" I tried hard to hide my nervousness.

"I'm going to study archaeology, just like my dad. He used to be the curator of the Rockefeller Museum." He looked at me. This time, I was the one with the considerate expression. "I practically grew up in that place, wandering the halls, looking at the scrolls. My dad worked his whole life on those scrolls, and he hoped to be able to crack the code. Now, it's up to me. I will be the one to uncover the next discovery."

"Which next discovery?" I asked, confused.

"Have you heard of the Dead Sea Scrolls?"

"I've heard of them, but I'm embarrassed to say I don't know much about them."

"It's a great story. The stuff legends are made from." He sat forward, casually putting his elbows on his knees. "A great example of how academic egos can get in the way of the truth."

His movements were naturally nonchalant, and he seemed so sure of himself, almost arrogant. The combination of his good looks and self-confidence was captivating.

"I'm intrigued..." I said, and catching myself, I added, "by this story."

"I don't blame you. It's a good story." His mouth lifted teasingly at the corners, and then he proceeded to tell the story. "Back in the 1940s, two discoveries were made a few years apart from each other. The amazing thing is that for years before that, archaeologists, crusaders, Templars, scoured the land and found nothing. Zilch. Zero. *Bubkes*. But then, coincidentally, a farmer in Nag Hammadi, and a shepherd boy in the caves around Qumran, in the area of the Dead Sea, found these ancient scrolls. They became known as the Dead Sea Scrolls." Shai looked at me, gauging my interest, then confidently continued. "In the first few years after they were found, the scrolls changed hands, each more corrupt than the next. They were sold to an antiques dealer, who put them in an old Bata shoebox. Then the story gets pretty crazy. He tried to sell them, but no one wanted to buy them because they thought that it must be a hoax. So he took out a full-page ad in an American newspaper, offering them to the highest bidder! Real ancient antiquities!" His hands, which had been busy gesticulating as he spoke, came to a stop momentarily, his fingers intertwined in front of him. "Well, no one wanted to get involved, because there's all this tension in the Middle East; no one wanted to get in the cross-fire between Egypt, Jordan and Israel."

"Why?"

"It's a funny coincidence. The timing that these scrolls were found was right when the Second World War had finished. All the Jews from Europe had no homes to go back to, and this country became both a mother and a father to thousands of orphans. All of those scared and scarred people. Before that, the region had swapped hands so many times over the last few thousand years. Then in 1948, the British Mandate split the region up, parceling out areas to Israel, Jordan and Egypt. Then the fights began as to whose land this really is. Each side claims to have been here first, and each side is vying for proof. And that's the biggest coincidence—it's during this whole time of flux that the scrolls are uncovered. So, these scrolls sent shockwaves into the academic communities. In an undercover sting operation, a Mossad agent buys them. Spends a few thousand dollars for them! Real antiquities! They travelled clandestinely from one hand to the next before they finally found their home in the Rockefeller Museum in Jerusalem." He paused for dramatic effect.

"Wow," I said.

Shai nodded excitedly. "Yeah, I know. That's only the beginning. Once they're brought here, then begins the job of deciphering them. Most of the scrolls were rolled up parchment, hidden in clay pots. But one, called the Copper Scroll, was engraved on a copper plate. That's what my father was working on." Shai was becoming very animated as he spoke and his hands were flying around in excitement. "The copper plate is very difficult to decipher, because the writing was engraved on the copper then rolled up, like a scroll. That means that the ancient secrets are on the *inside* of the scroll. Opening it means heating the copper enough so that it becomes pliable, but not too much so as not to ruin it. It is a slow process. Yet, as they opened the copper scroll, they began to find something of extreme significance engraved into it—a list of secret sites where the vast treasure of the Temple was alleged to be buried." He stopped to take a breath and looked at me, obviously happy with the effect his story was having on me. I was sitting forward, hands under my chin, completely enraptured.

He continued, "What is most interesting, the root of my father's obsession, was not the whereabouts of the treasure, but the mention of a mysterious hidden scroll: The Book of Secrets." His eyes lit up as he said it.

"What is the Book of Secrets?" I asked, intrigued. I clapped my hands together, shook the sand off of them and pulled back the tendrils of hair that were tickling my face.

"It's hard to know exactly...until it's found, that is. My guess is that it reveals a code."

His enthusiasm was contagious and I found myself sitting forward, riveted by his every word. "A code? What do you think the code is?"

"A code about the *real* identity of what they call God."

"Why is that so important?"

"Because, after all these years, all the fighting...this God, that God... Yaweh, El, Allah, Jesus, each side thinks they are right, that their God is the 'right' god. In my opinion, it's a bunch of bullshit. There is no God. I want to make sure I find this code and prove that."

"So why you?" I asked. "Why does your dad think that you'll uncover the next scroll?"

"He used to say he was *this* close to cracking the code." His fingers pinched together. "He pursued it his whole life. That was before. Before it all changed."

Shai closed his eyes for a long time. They were still closed, but he continued speaking, "My dad had a stroke a few years ago. He's been in a coma ever since."

We didn't talk for a while. I didn't know what to say to him. I was so used to people giving me their condolences about my mother that I knew how insincere they could sound. So I simply sat silently beside him.

My thoughts jumped from Shai's story to Natalie's. How odd that I heard them both on the same day. Was there a connection between the scrolls and La Que Saba? I wondered if Natalie knew about the scrolls and if they had anything to do with her search. Maybe Natalie would find some keys to the paradox. What a mystery this was turning out to be.

The beat of the drums reached its apex. The dancers swirled, the hoops flew, and the jugglers twirled their flames. Shai and I sat side by side, silently watching the performance. I gazed at the sky and saw the moon, a big round orb, glowing strangely bright in the night sky. Slowly, we watched it disappear. A lunar eclipse.

I had seen that once before. I don't remember how old I was exactly, but I remember something about my mother's excitement. I didn't really know what to expect when she gently woke me and carried me down the stairs and out the door to look at the moon. Wrapped in my blanket, and nestled close to her, I caught the contagion of her enthusiasm. I mimicked the wonder in her voice, proclaiming its beauty. Now I saw that it really is wondrous. An empty shadow replaced the space where the moon had been. Then slowly, a silver thread of moon revealed itself on the other side.

The throbbing echo of the music joining the surf was overwhelming—spellbinding in its tempo, magnetizing in its cadence. I felt my body unifying with the beat, reciprocating to the vibration of the drums, matching the pattern of the waves. I closed my eyes and let the pounding and pulsating pour over me. My heart was palpitating in the progressive beat. Thump, thump, tac, tac. Thump, thump, tac. Thump, thump, tac, tac. Thump, thump, tac.

The sensation of touch brought me out of my trance. Somehow, Shai was sitting so close to me that our elbows were lightly grazing. Had he moved towards me without my noticing, or had I moved towards him?

"What are your plans while you're in Israel?" He turned to look at me as he asked.

I felt the heat rise to my face. The reason sounded illogical, even in my own head. How did I tell him that I wanted to go in search of an illusion?

"I think I'm going to Jerusalem," I answered.

"To the Old City? No, you can't go," he asserted.

The nerve! I had just met him and he was already telling me what I could and couldn't do! His smugness steeled my determination to go.

He looked at my astonished face and laughed. "It's not safe for a girl by herself there right now, that's all! You can go, but only if I take you."

"I don't want to go with anybody. I want to go explore it on my own," I established.

"Don't worry, I'll be a total gentleman. Unless, of course you don't want me to be." He teasingly winked.

I jabbed him in the arm, and he yelped like it hurt.

"No really, what do you want to go to Jerusalem by yourself for? Especially right now, when there are…tensions."

"Actually, well, it's because I met a woman on the flight. An author…" I made sure to stress the word "author" because I didn't want him to think I was flaky. "And she told me about this mysterious…"

"Oh, no. Don't tell me you're one of those!" he interrupted, in mock horror.

"One of what?"

"Please, don't tell me you have the Messiah illusions!"

"What? I don't think so… I don't even know what that is."

"There's this effect Jerusalem has on people. It's called the Jerusalem Syndrome. Every year, people come to Jerusalem believing they are Jesus, or Moses, or some prophet or another. They believe that the end of the world is coming, the apocalypse, and that they are the Messiah. You see them walking in the streets, wearing robes, sandals, carrying their 'magical' sticks with them. Please, tell me you're not one of those crazy people!" His eyes teased me playfully.

"No, I'm not some wing nut."

"Good. You're too pretty to be a wing nut."

I was grateful for the darkness hiding my reddening face, and I watched the drummers and dancers who were packing up to leave. The beat was winding down and we were left with only the steady hum of the sea.

"It's just, well, the author on my flight, she told me about this mystery. I know it sounds crazy, but she mentioned this woman called the Nevea." I looked at the sea to avoid his gaze.

"Oh no, not that shit again." He spat.

"What? What shit?"

"That stupid woman story. Every few years her name comes up and it always makes for trouble. I don't even think she exists. Bunch of hippie bullshit. I think it's just a ruse to get the left wing nut jobs to come and start shit up." His anger was escalating. He punctuated the air with his hands. "But if she is real, she'd better watch out. Those bullshit stories that she spreads are dangerous. She starts riots, and she is going to get arrested one of these days."

Shai was close to me now, so close that I could feel the heat from his body. It made the rest of my body cold. He must have sensed me shiver, or maybe that was just his excuse to put his arm around my shoulders and bring me closer. His touch was welcoming. With his arm wrapped around me, I felt myself relax, cajoled into comfort. I didn't bring up the Nevea again.

I didn't know how long we sat in the sand like that, with me nestled in his arms. We watched the ebb and flow of the tide rolling in, talking about our lives, our pasts, and our futures as he slowly stroked my arm and caressed my hair, bringing chills to my body that had nothing to do with the cool breeze despite the night's heat.

Traces of rising sunlight were beginning to light up the sky when we finally decided to go. With Shai's arm casually draped over my shoulder, we walked along the now almost deserted boardwalk. Every few steps, he would gently touch my side, close to my breast, sending a surge of electricity through me. He walked me to the entrance of the hotel, stopping to face me in the shadows of the building.

"When do you leave?" he asked.

"Friday."

"That's too bad. I'm on duty for the next few days." He paused. "Can I give you my phone number and if you decide to come to Israel again, I can show you Jerusalem?"

"Only if you give me a tour of the Rockefeller Museum, too."

"Deal." He smiled.

"Deal." I repeated.

As he handed me a paper with his number scribbled on it, he reached for my hand and interlaced his fingers with mine. The other hand he put at the nape of my neck. Bringing me close to him in a single definitive movement, he kissed me. I brought my free hand to the nape of his neck, tickling my fingers in his hairline. Neither of us seemed to want the night to end.

Finally, I mustered up my restraint and pulled away, our fingers still interlocked.

"Come, I'll walk you to your room," he offered, stepping towards the hotel.

"No, that's okay. That won't be necessary." I smiled, trying to be as calm and collected as I knew how.

"It's okay, Selena. I won't try anything on you. Just walk you up, that's all," he responded, giving me his killer smile.

When I didn't answer, he leaned down and kissed me again, longer, more intense, even more convincingly than the first time. My body lit from within. Every ounce of my being leaned into him, screamed into him, wanted to feel abandon with him. The pull was excruciatingly irresistible, and my desire for him threatened to override my reason. I fought the urge to acquiesce, to invite him up, knowing perfectly well that he would not stop at the door, that he would come into my room, touch me in just the right way and make me weak. And my body reacted, begging and pleading with me to let him. But, my logical mind took over. I pulled away from him.

"Selena." he said breathlessly. "Just like the moon, a part of you is always hidden."

With a final peck, I let go of his hand and stepped away from him. I steeled myself as I entered the revolving door, his number tucked tightly in my palm. As I walked into the lobby, I took a deep breath, anchored my shoulders and refused to look back at him. Once the elevator doors closed, I exhaled, slumped against the wall and clenched my legs, dousing the fire within me.

CHAPTER 8

Thursday night, September 29th
Old City of Jerusalem

"Who are you?" I asked the old woman as she sipped from her steaming tea. She waited a long time before answering me. From somewhere outside the apartment, the muezzin started chanting a call for prayer, and it reverberated through the closed window blinds, giving the room a sort of mystical quality. The air around us seemed still, but somewhere in the distance, I could hear people screaming.

"I have been known by many names; I have lived many lives. In this time of my life, you may call me Sophia." She gave a soft wink, as if she were sharing some private joke, a secret that only she and I were privy to.

I felt as if I were being given a riddle to solve. Sophia exuded a sort of other-worldliness that I had never encountered before; yet, it felt familiar somehow. Being in her apartment felt as natural to me as being in an overgrown garden, with sweet perfumes, the flora of gentle petals and the comfort and sway of leaves on a shade tree. I sat on the sofa, leaning on one of the many beautifully brocaded cushions. Sophia sat on the delicately carved and ornate divan. Her long white tunic was loosely cinched at the waist with a golden cord; the lapel, embossed with maroon threaded designs of leaves and pomegranates, coiled its way around her neck. Her silver-white hair was escaping a low braid and her glimmering brown eyes were rimmed in kohl. She wore no jewelry, no adornments but carried a nobility about her. Sitting there on her divan, she looked like an ancient queen. Completely enraptured, I sat in front of her, waiting to hear what she would say next. It took a while.

She straightened her tunic across her knees before speaking again. "Every human is much like all the water contained in one raindrop. Each cell has the form of the whole. A single raindrop has within it many different life forms, each with its own microbes, each with its own physical characteristics, and though they have no contact with each other, they exist within the single drop. Just as each drop holds within it the form of the ocean. You have seen the soul of the world. You have been the raindrop that falls in the river, that flows to the sea, that is pulled by the sun into a cloud. You have carried all the wisdom of the rain, the river and the sea. Just like the raindrop, you have returned again and again."

"So is that the second Sacred Sphere? That everything is part of the whole?"

"The Second Sphere correlates with the Third. The entire universe is made of correspondence and vibration."

"What does that mean?" I asked, crossing my legs under me. I felt like I was under the tutelage of an ancient oracle. I had never really known an older woman, never been given sage advice before. Even my mother was more of a contemporary than an older, wiser woman. I felt comforted being here with Sophia, especially because of what was happening outside. What sounded like a loud pop ripped through the air, so close, I was sure it must have been just outside the window. What followed was the sound of many pairs of boots running. A few anguished screams reached in, making the hair on the back of my neck stand on end. The collective screams dissipated, but two continued. I heard the cries of a child in pain and the anguished wails of her mother. Tear gas, I assumed. The thought made me shudder. I covered my ears and shook my head from side to side, imploring the noise to stop. Eventually, more voices came, and it sounded like the child and her mother were being carried away. I was petrified. I knew the hour was getting late and I hoped that she would allow me to stay, at least until the rioting stopped.

I don't know if she sensed my fear, but the Nevea was calm and unbothered, as if this little chat we were having was perfectly normal, under perfectly normal circumstances. Once the streets were again quiet and I had removed my hands from my ears and relaxed a bit, she continued.

"It means you must Engage your Energy. All women and men, all living creatures are connected by an energy, which is the raw material from which the universe was built. The energy cannot be manipulated; rather, it leads us gently forward. If we try to reverse its direction, to control it, we become fearful, because this energy is free and wild. You radiate your energy in a field all around you."

"Like an aura?"

Sophia smiled and nodded. "Yes, little bird. All humans radiate what they are. You can radiate conflict and anger or harmony and serenity. Every human, every thing, has a field of energy that surrounds them. That energy field can interact with the energy field of those around them. In the near future, new corridors of energies will open in the universe."

"Are you referring to the energy that can be harnessed into electricity?" I asked, thinking of the new initiatives in reusable energy and sustainability, like harnessing solar energy or hybrid cars.

"That is part of the answer, yes, but it is only a by-product of the change to come, not the solution. For many years now, humanity has felt as if it was waiting for instructions, but didn't understand what it was waiting for. The energy bodies in the universe, as well as your physical bodies will soon morph. The DNA structure of your body will change the way in which it communicates with your consciousness. The energy pulsating in the universe will resonate with your awareness and with your understanding. The universal energy will awaken centers of your being. That which you are seeks balance with that which you will become."

"So, I'll have magical powers?" I asked, skeptically picturing myself as a magician, raising my energy levels to the point of illumination, like a light bulb.

"Much simpler, little bird. Everything will have magical powers. Everything that exists is energy. This table, this cup, the tea within it, even you, are made of energy. You are a mirror of all that ever was, is and will be. You carry the light of the highest vibration. You have the potential for the highest form of creation."

"Like the principles of matter in quantum physics?"

"Quite. Much like the uncertain world of matter, everything exists in pure potential before it conforms to the three dimensional world of your awareness. So your awareness can change the reality of matter."

"So, what does that have to do with *my* energy? How do I make any changes to the reality of matter?" I remembered watching a show in which a man claimed to bend a spoon with the powers of his mind. I always figured it was a clever trick of the eye, a well-rehearsed deception.

"You create the bridge between possibility and form."

I squinted, trying to follow what she was telling me, but failing. "What does that mean?"

"Through the process of irradiation..."

"What? Radiation?" I jumped in, thinking of the months of treatment my mother's tumor received, only to leave her weak and hairless.

"Not radiation, which is a poison that kills your cells. Irradiation, also known as 'blessing' in all the spiritual traditions, is the technique of charging yourself with new and positive energy. That is the energy that exists within you, the energy that engages with the universal energy of the highest potential. To keep that energy contained only within yourself would lead to spiritual congestion. All good things must be circulated, not stored. You must engage your energy and then share it with others."

"How do I do that?" I asked, tilting my head to the side in contemplation.

"You must send the energy, the radiant pulse of blessing, love to all beings, compassion to all beings, joy to all beings and serenity to all beings."

I raised an eyebrow. "Okay, I mean, that sounds lovely and all. But how does that engage my energy? I mean, isn't that just me sending good thoughts out? A noble endeavor, for sure, but if people don't want to feel joy, or love, or anything I send them, it really doesn't do much good, does it?"

"Not only is it a noble endeavor, it is the essential element. Your true essence, your center of consciousness is free. It is your natural state, the way you were meant to be. Engaging your energy means harnessing that power, coalescing it into the material realm. You see, energy is always in motion, ever changing and transforming. The elements of energy vibrate at variable speeds. The energy that exists within the realm of physical creation, that of form, vibrates very slowly. On the other hand, the energy that exists in the spiritual creation, that of possibility, vibrates very quickly. Engaging your energy simply means creating energy that vibrates at the speed of possibility rather than form. What was previously only a possibility becomes form. Energy is your creation. But it must be congruent with a supernal vibration. As with the Hermetic axiom…"

"The what?" I interrupted, resisting the urge to get my notebook out to write all of this down. It was a lot to take in, but I was intrigued to hear the rest.

"The Hermetic axiom, named after Hermes Trismegistus…"

"Hermes who?" I repeated.

"Hermes Trys-mah-geest-us. It means 'Thrice Great.' He was a great philosopher, mystic and alchemist. The folklore tells that they are his words on the *Tabula Smaragdina,* The Emerald Tablet, that gives us the Hermetic axiom of *'As below, so above; and as above, so below. With this knowledge alone you may work miracles.'* But, in fact, the Emerald Tablet existed long before it fell into the hands of Hermes. The wisdom of the Emerald Tablet is primordial."

"So, what happened to this Emerald Tablet? Where did it go?"

"Ahhh, that my dear little bird is a great story to be told. The wisdom of the tablet was handed down a long lineage, a wisdom that came to the very beginnings of humanity. Many would love to know of its current whereabouts. Many wars and crusades have been waged in the pursuit of finding it. Which is the reason that Sarah, upon finding the tomb of Hermes in Hebron and uncovering the tablets, ensured that the oral tradition would never be lost, even if the men would wage wars over its possession. In the women's tents, Sarah would teach the Universal wisdom, and with it they would gain all the knowledge and all the magic of the Universe."

I was intrigued. In my imagination, I pictured sitting at the foot of an ancient wise woman. I longed to be a part of those nomadic days, traveling with a tribe of women, listening to the wisdom of our foremothers. And, then it dawned on me, I actually was.

"So, how does this wisdom, this magic, work? What does it all mean in day to day life?"

"Quite simply, it means that the experiences of your daily lives are reflections of the events occurring in the cosmos. Human beings, in fact, all living things, are a coalescence of energy connected to every other living thing in the world. This pulsating energy is the essence of your being and the being of the universal consciousness."

"Like a cosmic mirror?"

She laughed. "Yes, quite, little bird. Except that the frequency, the resonance, the charge emitted, if you will, created in the cosmos is of a much higher, faster vibration. As it lowers into the physical elements, the lower dimensions, it becomes slower, less charged. So the divine energy mirrors the physical energy, but at an exponentially higher vibration."

"Like a two-sided mirror?" I asked, thinking of the mirror my roommate used, the one that flipped from a normal sized reflection to the other side, which magnified my face many times its size. This was not always a good thing.

"Much like a magnified image, yes, except that instead of the overall image becoming magnified, each impulse in that image becomes magnified. And the magnification is infinite, unbound by the constraints of the mirror. Picture an entire web of invisible string, tying your every thought, every impulse to its counterpart in the cosmos. Every thought, every action, every impulse already exists in a field of possibility."

I straightened up, conscientious of my every thought and action. I tried to bring myself to the place of serenity that I had felt earlier in the evening, but try as I might, it was to no avail. I just couldn't turn my questions off. "So, how do I engage my energy then? If I'm a physical being, don't I just vibrate at the physical level?"

"To engage your energy, you must learn to align your energy with the energy of possibility. The seed of anything exists in consciousness first, and the fulfillment of anything already exists in the cosmos. It takes the form of potential then awakens desire within you. If you are unaware of your energy, then you assume your desire awoke by itself. If you recognize that desire can only come by reflecting the vibration of its form in the cosmos, your impulses, thoughts and actions will reflect that form."

"Are you saying that everything already exists?" I asked, uncrossing my legs and pointing my feet in front of me, rotating them at the ankles. I stretched my arms above my head, attempting to release the tension in my jawbone before clasping my hands behind my neck. It did nothing to relieve the tightness of my clenched jaw.

"In the form of energy, yes."

"And that there is an established design in the universe?" I continued.

She nodded patiently. "Yes."

"Hasn't modern science proven that some things are part of evolution? That the creation of the world happened by chaotic chances, not by some grand design?"

"Science has proven that the world was created by a contraction, from nothing, and the contraction created an exquisitely intense energy, a powerful light."

"Big bang theory, right?" I asked.

"Calling it the 'big bang' would imply there was only one."
She chuckled.

"So, what was there if not the big bang?"

"There was an intention."

"As in creationism? Hasn't Darwin and the theory of evolution disproved the creation story as just a myth?" I asked, feeling more comfortable with science, biology and reason, with things that could be measured.

"Yes, creation as told in myth is simply a metaphor. Taken literally it represents a one-sided view of the universe; however, the theory of evolution is equally as myopic."

"How so?" I asked, uncomfortable with buying the creation story. After all, the right-wing religious nut jobs would love nothing more than to convince us that the world was really made in seven days, rather than through millions of years of evolution.

"Evolution exists, of course," she answered me, as if reading my thoughts once again. "But so does creation. The premise of survival of the fittest was built on the faulty assumption that the world is competitive, or hierarchically based, a comfortable explanation for a world based in hierarchy. But that is the illusion of the collective ego. The hierarchical structure of humanity sees that there is a God that has dominion over man, and that man has dominion over woman, animal and child. And that is why you have a world steeped in domination. But, stories have always revealed certain truths that science could not. Stories comprise the riddles that lead humanity to scientific breakthroughs. Remember that Darwin, too, was a great student of the stories. Even Darwin, in the waning moments of his life, between fits of relentless vomiting, as his suffering was ending and he was faced with the prospect of death, even with his last breath, Darwin was compelled to cry out, 'My God!'"

I imagined Darwin lying on his deathbed. What must he have seen in those last moments? What wisdom must have crept into his overly evolved mind? Did he have any regrets? Would he have done things differently?

The vision made me remember my mother's last days in the hospital. She had grown weak; the radiation and chemotherapy had taken their toll. The doctor asked to speak to me privately and pulling me into the hallway, out of her earshot, he informed me that she had days to live. But she knew. The hardest part was facing her with this knowledge, sitting by her bedside as if the doctor's words had never been spoken, as if it were not true. But my mother knew, and in those few days, she tried to prepare me. *"Live a full life,"* she had said. *"Don't let any opportunity pass you by, allow yourself to be surprised where life may take you."*

At the time, I thought I was doing what she told me to do by going to school and working, making something of myself. Yet, now, as I sat here with Sophia, I realized she meant much more than just that.

"So Darwin's theory of evolution is not correct?" I asked, once I'd brought my attention back to the conversation.

"Even Darwin could not escape the male-dominated society of the nineteenth and twentieth centuries." Sophia's endearingly contagious laugh made me laugh, too.

"What do you mean?"

"In his epic tome to evolution, Darwin also explained in detail his theory of Sexual Selection. The scientific community of the time first ignored it, then called it blasphemy and heresy, then condemned it, then ridiculed, criticized and re-ignored it. Only in the last few decades has it been re-examined and accepted as self-evident."

"Why?"

"Because sexual selection is an incredibly powerful concept that puts a lot of importance on women and their ability to influence evolution. This was simply too much for the religiously minded, patriarchal society to admit to."

"What were they scared of?"

"Well, scientists are now finding out that it is the specific selection by women that guides humanity towards a specific destination."

"So the old world misogyny kept women from having power because of the theory of evolution?" I asked, incensed.

"The evolutionary path of humanity and the theory of evolution are distinct."

"How so?" I sputtered.

Sophia continued, "The theory exposed a truth that was always there and much has been revealed since the hypothesis came to light. But, even evolution theory has its limitations. The theory bridges the gap of understanding of how the environment has changed humanity, but it doesn't explain the dynamic force that we, as humans, have on our environment. As scientists are now learning, there exists a force that lies beyond the physical, beyond the world of the senses, beyond the material world. There comes a point at which physical scientists, as far into their research as they have come, must throw their hands up in despair. Every scientific discovery allows for the next spiritual secret to be revealed. And every spiritual secret has been encoded in the stories that have been told by the Story Women. The past and present are enfolded into a future that is unfolding. Science and the Secrets are twin sisters, joined at the hip. Where one goes, the other follows. We, the Story Women, just had to wait until science caught up to reveal our stories."

"So, the Story Women knew about twenty first century science?" I asked, so incredulous that my eyes widened. Everything she was saying seemed so mystical and magical, and I wanted to listen to her, but the skeptical part of me just wouldn't shut-up.

"The Story Women only revealed each code when humanity was ready. Scientists knew only what knowledge was shown to them, little bird. The secrets were written as codes and the first code was written into the story of creation, into the first book written by man. In that book, it says that God was projected in numbers, letters and sounds. Everything that has ever lived, or will ever live, was a reflection of *elohim*. That includes any thought or any action. Humans, animals, amoebas, everything is a reflection of *elohim*. But, the creation of this world is only one aspect of the origin of the Universe.

The word *elohim*, literally means 'master of prospect and possibility.' Quantum scientists have been busy trying to decipher the concept of prospect and possibility, encrypted in those codes. And as they do, more secrets are revealed."

"So is this about God? Because, I really don't think I believe in God. Throughout history, wars have been waged in the name of God." I was getting flustered, but continued, "God's authority has dictated how people live their lives, what they eat and how they dress. God has been the reason for so much of the world's hatred."

"It is not how it has been interpreted. *Elohim* means Gods and Goddesses. It is plural and has no gender. 'God' is an ambiguous word in human language because it appears to refer to something that is known, but the transcendent is unknowable and unknown. 'God' is beyond names and forms. The best things cannot be told in words because they transcend all thought."

"But the story of creation is from religion..." I stammered, trying to explain my reasoning, making sure that she knew that I didn't subscribe to any dogmatic view of religious structure. I thought of all those religious people who became devout followers, then like missionaries, trying to turn everyone to see things from their view and perceived everybody else as wrong. Then they got fanatical, thinking they'd found the answers and tried to oppress and convert all those around them. They made laws to force others to accept their answers. They built temples and courts for what they considered the absolute truths and became imprisoned by them. They became enslaved to their religion.

"This is a truth higher than religion. This is living at a new level of understanding, enjoying higher kinds of awareness. That is the path of the mystic."

"What is the path of the mystic? Isn't that just more religion?"

"The mystical path is not religion, though all religions have mystical secrets. This is the awareness that was the original intention of the stories. This is an awakening of a slumber that humanity has been in for much too long. There is no conflict with the spiritual elements in any religion; in fact, on the deepest level, harmony exists between the world's teachings. It is simply that much emphasis has been placed on blind faith in a God, rather than a true understanding of the nature of 'God.' God is merely the code for who we are. Encoded in us is a reflection of the Universe, and the Universe is a reflection of us. Religion calls it by the word 'God,' scientists refer to it as the observer, mystics call it light, spirituality calls it creator, naturalists call it nature and physicists call it the quantum field. It doesn't matter what name you feel comfortable with, you know your truth."

"Can I say universal mind? The power that exists, separate from my material reality? Like mind over matter?" I queried, trying to make sense of what she was teaching me, trying to make the irrational rational.

Sophia nodded, smoothing her hair back with wrinkled fingers. "You can attribute your understanding to absolutely anything, and you will always be right. Every impulse has within it the range of possibility. Thought itself draws impulses to it like metal to a magnet, a magnetic interchange between visible and invisible worlds. Do you know how lightening works, little bird?"

"Yeah, sure. Lightening makes a bright light from the sky and thunder makes a loud noise. Boom." I grinned.

"Lightening doesn't actually come from the sky; rather, it is an electrical impulse that searches for a current to connect to. When the electrical charge from above meets its equivalent from the ground, the two make an explosive connection and create a phenomenal display of light."

I pursed my lips together. "Really? I didn't know that. So you're saying that it's the same as thought?"

"Yes, lightening, thoughts, desires—all searching for their equivalent." She made a flurry with her hands, finally connecting the fingers in a loud clap. "This magnetic interchange is the dichotomy between the union of male and female, active and passive energies. The impulse is proportionate to the intensity of the thought. Just as a flower dies, but its scent lives on, the thought impulse makes itself felt in the ether; therefore, one person may impress herself on her own epoch. That influence is carried between the two worlds of visible and invisible, from one succeeding age to another until it affects a large portion of humankind. So you see, little bird, there is no such thing as mind over matter. Mind *is* matter."

"In one of my college classes, we learned Descartes's philosophy, *cogito ergo sum;* I think, therefore, I am. Is that what you mean?"

"Let us say instead; *sum ergo cogito;* I am, therefore, I think. The ultimate truth of who you are is not I AM this or that, it is simply—I AM." She paused for a few moments, and I let the energy of her words fall on me. My mind reeled as it tried to find a way to counter this concept, but every turn in my mind took another turn, which boggled my senses even more.

She gave me a few minutes of repose before continuing. "The material realm exists only in the perception of the energy within which it is occupied. Matter is an illusion. The space between the sun and the earth must be filled with a material medium, astral light, which produces enormous vibration and causes friction. Friction generates electricity, a correlative of magnetism, which forms the tremendous forces on Earth. The light itself is a creation, an energy that produces heat by friction. So you see, little bird, everything is energy. Nothing is solid. Everything vibrates at a different speed, and though it appears solid to the human eye, under a microscope, that same solid object reveals molecules vibrating at almost the speed of light."

"If light is a creation, and energy is light, does that mean I can just create more energy for the things that I want to happen?"

Sophia shook her head. "Energy cannot be created or destroyed. It can only be transformed. Just like the energy that we call light. When the energy of the light increases, it produces higher and faster vibrations of light in the ether. As the vibrations become shorter and weaker, the waves of light slow down, creating what we perceive as darkness. All thought is also a form of energy, but a thought of 'truth' has a higher rate of vibration, while a thought of 'error' has a weak vibration."

"Can't we just start thinking new thoughts? Invent new behavior patterns? Won't that create new energy?"

"If you wish to change a behavior pattern, you cannot destroy it; you can only transform it into another behavior pattern. Just like if you wish to change your thoughts, you must transform the old negative thoughts into new positive ones."

"How do I change the negative connotation of the past into a positive energy for the future?" I asked, thinking of all the chaos happening outside. I listened intently for any noise from outside, but it was eerily silent. The silence scared me more than the occasional shouts. I worried that I would hear another tear gas flare. A shiver of fear trickled down my spine.

"Chaos is the catalyst for change. The devolutionary path has led us to a worldwide breakdown, and the evolutionary path can bring us to a world of peace, harmony, wellbeing and sustainability. Now is the time for humanity to reunite and become a single nation once again." She gingerly straightened her skirt about her knees, taking a deep breath as her fingers smoothed the linen fabric. The movement calmed me. "By rebuilding into a united humanity, we will also rebuild our connection to Nature."

The discussion reminded me of a story I'd heard once. When Mother Theresa was asked to attend an anti-war rally, she answered that she would never attend an anti-war rally, she would only join a pro-peace rally. As if highlighting my thoughts, a spray of bullets rang out in the nearby streets. I jumped and my breathing halted for a moment. Once I'd caught my breath, I asked, "How can we possibly get to the evolutionary path?"

"The time has come to balance transcendent spirituality, the spirituality that exists outside of ourselves, with immanent spirituality, the spirituality that exists within us. The time has come to invoke the Divine Feminine, but not as a supreme deity that exists outside of humanity. Goddess as energy, as a co-creative reality, manifested immanently. Goddess, or any deity, is a form of spiritual energy that attaches itself to a human concept. If humans perceive that form of energy, the energy becomes real. Just like the ever-expanding universe, the energy we perceive changes the perception of the universe. What we believe becomes real. And what is real, we believe."

PART II

THE GIFT OF KNOWLEDGE

And the power of the powers by my gnosis
Of the angels who have been sent by my word
And the gods in their seasons by my command,
And it is with me that the spirits of all humans exist,
And it is within me that women exist.

—Thunder, Perfect Mind
From the scrolls found at Nag Hammadi

CHAPTER 9

Thursday morning, September 29ᵗʰ
Tel Aviv

In some deeper part of me, I knew it was only a dream, but it unnerved me nonetheless. I saw myself as if simultaneously above myself and within myself, naked, sprawled on a bed of soft leaves, waiting for something, though I didn't know for what. And then the limitless pleasure started, the strong pulsating pull of temptation. I wracked my body to dull the sensation, but my movements merely intensified the feelings. I was in a lush, aromatic garden, and the lingering scent of juniper and lilac intoxicated me. The air around me reverberated, like being underwater, though it might have been the echo of my beating heart. It was a place that might have been forever, yet no time, a lost horizon of my own soul. And then, serpentine and molten, I felt something slithering up to me. I sensed eyes on me. Eyes so perceptive and piercing that a chill ran down my spine. Eyes that belied some sort of secret, some lost language, some inside joke. Smiling eyes. Intrepid eyes. Devious eyes.

I woke up with a jolt and tried to clear my mind. The long, luxurious shower did little to help. I should have been tired, having only gotten into bed in the wee hours of the morning.

But, meeting Shai had energized me. I'd barely gotten any sleep at all.

Shai. The thought of him made me shiver. It was rare for me to get so worked up about a man, and back home, I'd hardly dated at all. The guys my age were so immature, only interested in sports and drinking. It seemed infantile to talk about superficial things, the latest fad, party, or gossip. I didn't really have much in common with the boys my age, or the girls, for that matter.

But being with Shai had felt different. He had depth and saw life through a different lens. I stretched my arms above my head, leaving them hanging above me like a limp marionette. Recreating our time together in my mind made me smile, and I spontaneously emitted a giggle. I pictured his long fingers in my hair, the way he looked at me, how beautiful he'd made me feel. The thought made me remember Natalie. She was probably used to people looking at her that way, used to seeing her beauty through their eyes.

I stood, dripping over my suitcase, trying to figure out what to wear, but the contents were dull variations of the same old style. No beautiful blue dresses, no dangling earrings, no jingling bracelets. My wardrobe was monochromatic. Colorless and efficient. I decided on a pair of jeans and a white t-shirt. I grabbed my backpack, slipped on some runners and went for breakfast.

It was still early and except for the few wait staff, the hotel's breakfast buffet was empty. I loaded my plate and picked up a copy of the Jerusalem Post. *'Bomb Attack; Peace Process Threatened,'* one headline read; *'Violence Escalating in Jerusalem,'* screamed another. Underneath the headlines were the smiling faces of the Chairman and the Prime Minister, shaking hands with each other, while the American President stood, smiling proudly behind them. I put the paper down. More of the same news—negotiations stalled, parties losing faith, promises broken, threats of attack.

I began to reconsider going to Jerusalem. Maybe it would be smarter to stay in Tel Aviv, maybe even stay inside the relative safety of the hotel for the two day layover. I ripped the picture out of the paper and placed it in a fresh page of my notebook. The notebook had been a gift from my favorite teacher while my mom was still sick. It was my saving grace through many months of hospital visits, through the anguish I felt at losing her. It was where I shared my deepest thoughts and unspoken regrets. It was also where I had glued the picture of my mom with the smiling man and the letters I had found. Despite its humble appearance, the notebook, filled and tattered, with its spiral binding unwinding and tan cover graying, was my therapy, my catharsis, my solace.

Still on a high from last night's encounter with Shai, I turned to the page where the letters and picture were glued down. I thought of the man in the picture, with his kind eyes and dark curls, so much like my own. The first letter, a thinned, folded paper with creases worn from use was still in the envelope, dated seven months before my birth. There was no return address. On the front of the envelope was my mother's name, but the forwarding address was through the Peace Corps mailing system. The zigzag-edged stamp portrayed an ancient silver coin, with the word *Liban* etched into it, and some script in what I assumed was Arabic. The handwriting was beautifully decorative, a work of careful calligraphy. The D of my mother's name crafted to look like a musical note, rich with tone.

> *Ma Chérie Deborah,*
>
> *It saddened me to the core of my being to hear of your departure, though I know it is best that you left. The only thing I can't understand is why you didn't say goodbye, but I am sure you have your reasons.*
>
> *The war here has taken a new ferocity and it delights my heart to think of you safe in America. I only wish that I will soon see you again.*
>
> *As for this rampant and raging place, the situation is only becoming even more repugnant. The insurgents have infiltrated the civilian population. The streets are no longer safe. Even the airport has been ransacked and barricaded, and it was fortunate you left when you did. The curfew established by the military is foreboding, though the incursions occur at all hours of day and night. Whosoever has the money and resources to leave is leaving, while the people who are most at risk remain. My biggest concern is for the well-being of the children, who are falling prey to indoctrination by the radical factions. Our work here is needed now more than ever. I cannot bring myself to imagine how I will accomplish this without you, but, my love, I will try to do what I can in your honor and with your usual spirit.*

Darling Deborah, I miss you so. I only hope that this letter finds you safe. I look forward to holding you in my arms once again, to seeing your beauty radiate upon me. The longing I feel for you is tempered only by the notion that you are out of harm. That, my dear, is my greatest solace amidst all this devastation.

Please, write to me and allow me to know you have made it to safety.

I look forward to your letter. In the meantime, I dream of you.

Yours truly,

M

P.S. Mon âme te cherchera à tout jamais.

Every time I read the letter, the scar of my loneliness reopened. This side of my mother was a mystery to me. I had never known what she did during her involvement with the peace organization, and I had certainly never known her to be adventurous and spirited. I had never known there was a man who loved her as honestly, as completely as M did, whoever M was. The pang of loneliness overwhelmed me again. Why hadn't my mom shared this information with me? Why had she kept this secret to herself? I resisted the urge to get really mad, resisted the temptation to think bad of her. I felt ashamed to think of her with blame and criticism. After all, according to M, she was doing good work, making the world a better place. But, then I couldn't understand why she would keep M a secret from me. I wished I could have had just one more opportunity to ask her.

On the front cover of my notebook were the words from Gandhi—"Be the change you wish to see in the world." I thought of the graffiti I had seen the night before: *Know Peace.* A notion materialized in my mind. Combining the graffiti's message with Gandhi's words would make: Be the peace you wish to see in the world. I sipped my coffee, lost in my thoughts.

On a fresh page I scribbled:

> *What does it mean to know peace?*
>
> *How can we experience this knowledge?*
>
> *How can we 'be' peace?*
>
> *How can we hope for peace without knowing peace when the headlines of every newspaper in the world scream that peace is in crisis?*
>
> *When politicians engage us in wars we don't want to fight.*
>
> *When society establishes roles that keep some members inferior.*
>
> *When religions breed fanatics.*
>
> *We can't possibly know that peace can exist. We keep thinking in relation to it not being possible. We keep thinking of what war feels like, what attacks to retaliate for, who is right and who is wrong.*
>
> *But we don't know peace.*
>
> *We need to know peace.*
>
> *I need to know peace.*

I remembered my favorite teacher, the one who gave me the notebook, once talking about Gandhi's philosophy of *satyagraha,* the positive transformational energy, or 'truth force'. The goal was to become aware of the constructive force, to transform conflict rather than to suppress it or have it explode into violence. I remember she told me that changes in structure must be preceded by changes in function. Just like she had said, you cannot sit in the corner of a round room, so can you not find peace in conflict. To change the structure of society, we must change the old ways of thinking, feeling and acting. Likewise, in order to change the structure of our behavior, we must also change our old ways of thinking, feeling and acting. It seemed that in this region of the world, there was always an explosion of violence, a perpetual cycle of conflict.

I decided that I was going to try to take my teacher's, and Gandhi's, advice. I willed myself to try to *know* peace. I was determined to feel at peace, to resonate with peace. I was going to *be* the peace I wished to see in the world.

I decided that I would go to Jerusalem. Besides, it might be the last time I would have the chance.

CHAPTER 10

Thursday night, September 29ᵗʰ
Old City of Jerusalem

The streets beyond the apartment had grown quiet in the twilight hours. Now that the storm of violence seemed to be over, I considered leaving and making my way back to Tel Aviv. No sooner had I thought that did I hear a low flying helicopter circling above, reminding me of the danger outside.

"Shall I tell you the parable of Spiderwoman?"

I could tell she was trying to distract me from the noise. It wasn't working, but she continued nonetheless.

"The Spiderwoman, who created the web of life, gave a little spider a mission—to collect all the wisdom of the world and bring it back to her. In exchange, the little spider would be called 'the wisest of all time.' Smugly, the little spider replied that he could do it in a mere three days. He collected all the wisdom in the world and put it into a large, black pot. He tied the pot to his back and started to climb to the sky, slowly scaling a tall coconut tree, the apex of which was lost in the clouds. When he finally reached the top, the little spider was so pleased with himself that he threw his two forward legs up into the air in triumph. The weight of the pot caused his other legs to lose their grip and he fell back down to the ground. The pot broke and all of the wisdom was scattered amongst the farthest reaches of the world."

"And the moral of the story is that the whole world has its wise traditions?"

Sophia titled her head back in that laughing gesture that I found so alluring. It was so genuine that it made her look like a living goddess and a loving grandmother at the same time. "The moral of the story is that many, many years ago, a truth so powerful, so evocative, was threatening the established rulers. To protect the wisdom contained within the Spheres, emissaries were sent to the furthest reaches of the Earth: Tibet, Peru, India, the Americas, the Pacific Islands, the Northern people, nowhere on Earth did the wisdom not reach. The secrets were encoded, hidden, and the people were instructed to wait; wait for the signal to release the wisdom."

"Why don't people know this? Why haven't people told anyone this?" I asked.

"You live in an age of information. You have much knowledge, but you lack wisdom. Most people today say they are thinking, but in fact, they are information shuffling."

I thought of my college courses. It was true that most of the courses were variations on reading and interpreting something that someone else wrote. Alternative thinking was discouraged, and the goal of the educational system seemed to be to churn out well-rehearsed peons of corporate culture.

"It makes me think of the schools of higher learning, all the intellectual elites vying for more wisdom," I said sardonically, not even trying to hide the tongue-in-cheekiness.

"Knowledge alone cannot reveal wisdom. I invite you to expand beyond the intellect. To come into knowledge with the divine."

The word "divine" triggered something within me. I stumbled over my thoughts and a familiar unease crept in. It was the same discomfort I felt around people who were overcome with their religious fervor. The same feeling I got around people who saw divisions around their beliefs and judged me for mine. The unease that came with being told what the right way to think is, the right thing to believe. The word "divine," used so often by the careless nurse whose job it was to take care of my mom—*"It's the divine will,"* she would say, or, *"It's in the hands of the divine."* As if that should answer the question of—why? The churning in my stomach made me want to get up and bolt out the door.

But then I remembered the chaos outside and it held me in place.

"Ah, the song the sparrow learns in its youth is the song it sings for life," Sophia remarked. "You learned to doubt and fear in your youth, and you keep whistling the same tune."

"I don't think I sing a song of fear," I answered defiantly.

"The ancient wisdom traditions teach that there are two fundamental emotions: love and fear. All other emotions are rooted in one or the other. Fear is faith in negative things and negative circumstances. Fear will have you believe you are surrounded by a hostile universe, filled with hostile beings, ready and waiting to prey on you and destroy you. Fear will have you believe that the Divine has somehow orchestrated the negative illusions of life. Do you see the idiocy in that?"

"Okay," I argued as I shifted from a cross-legged position to a prone position, like a ready debater. "Then how do you explain that divinity allows what's happening outside right now?" I pointed to the world beyond the windows. As if on cue, angry, barking men's yells imbued the air. In retaliation, bullet fire commanded the sky. More yelling. More bullets. At least it was moving further away from us.

"It's alright, little bird, you will find that the greater the fear, the greater the power. You fear because your culture fears. But there are other tunes in this orchestra, other verses to this harmony. The cosmos is made up of a vast musical harmony, the harmony of the spheres. Notice the word you use for the universe is just that, a *uni*-verse, a single rhythm, one harmony exists in this universal multi-verse. But humankind has not always seen this world as a *uni*-verse. Your history has been one of division rather than unity. That was the illusion, the misinterpretation of the Sphere of Polarity. You see this world as a world of polarities, either this or that, right or left, good or evil. You divide everything. Even the two ends of the pole, the north and south, you consider as two divisions. But they are in essence merely two ends of the same pole, surrounded and hidden by masses of land. Do you think you can continue to stay divided and survive?"

"No, I guess not." I sat back, enfolded in the cushions. My head was spinning with so many thoughts vying for attention. I suddenly felt empty, winded, as if all the air had left my body. I nodded and listened, picturing the earth from above and all of humanity waving at me.

She sipped from her tea before continuing. "This has been the demise of your humanity, the story you have been telling yourselves for millennia. This was not always so. There was a time when we all knew the truth. That was a time of Nature. In those days, humanity's communication with Nature, and each other, flowed. Words were not even necessary, and people would communicate with their thoughts and intentions. It was a time of unity, and the whole of humanity was like a single nation. In those days, people did not know that they could be separated from Nature, nor did they want to be."

"What changed?"

Sophia raised her eyebrows, smiled and opened her arms in a wide circle, like she was calling together a class full of children. Her features lit up invitingly and she peered at me as if about to impart some long forgotten lesson. "A great shift occurred. Brutal conquerors invaded the peaceable existence. Hatred replaced love, war replaced peace, and Ego replaced Nature. People began to want to change Nature and use her for themselves. They grew detached from Nature, separated and alienated from her and from each other. The single nation of the ancient world became divided and splintered. That created confusion and chaos—*Bilbul.*"

"Like the Tower of Babel? Or Babylon?" The connection suddenly dawned on me.

"Exactly," she beamed at me like a proud school teacher to her favorite pupil. "The two elements of civilization clashed and the division between them grew. To protect the ego, the conquerors built a belief system based in fears. They convinced people that life is a lesson in sacrifice, a journey through hardships and toil.

They created worlds of illusion, cast shadows of doubt, built kingdoms of fear, shame and guilt. But life, my little bird, is none of those things. Do you see what life is?"

I considered this for a while, trying to figure out the right answer because I wanted her to look at me with adoration again. Finally, I said, "I don't really know. Can anyone know what life is?"

"If life is a gift then life is not about you, but you are about life." Her look embraced me in its warmth. Her voice was gentle, with that lilt that was imperceptible but charming beyond measure.

"Okay, if that's so, then what about hardships? Evil? Wars? Are they gifts?" I scoffed at the idea.

"They are part of the most desirable gift of all. The purpose of creation itself is to reach equivalence of form with the Nature of creation. It is only through this enhanced perception that you may become as wise as Nature itself. It is in the very process of uniting with Nature that you will feel as eternal and complete as Nature."

"I don't see how evil can be considered a gift." A cold shudder ran through me. It suddenly dawned on me how close to danger I had been in the streets, and how close I still may be once I left Sophia's home. I thought of all the warnings I had gotten about coming here, and looking back on it, I felt like an idiot. I had really gotten myself into a heap of trouble. The worry was overwhelming, but Sophia continued to talk in her soft lull, and soon I was taken in again by her words.

"E-v-i-l is simply a mirror reflection of l-i-v-e. It's like skating on a frozen pond. Above the ice is the live reality, and under the ice is the evil reality. It's easy to fall through the ice. It's easy to stay under, easier than trying to climb back up to the live reality. Sometimes you need help to come back up. Sometimes it's easier to stay under and live in fear, doubt and shame. *That* is the evil reality. The choice of consciousness is your greatest gift. If you believe you are a victim of a chaotic and unjust world, then chaos and injustice will become your reality. You will be right. And you will be miserable. If you choose to rise above the dark consciousness and separate evil illusion from reality, you will control your destiny and live in that reality."

"Wasn't the Tower of Babel a story about sin and destruction?" I asked.

She looked at me, but I couldn't assess her expression.

"What do you know about sin?" she asked.

The question took me aback because I didn't know if she was asking rhetorically or referring to something I did.

"What do you mean?" I asked. My mind scrambled with thoughts of all of the things I had done wrong in life. And then, fearing that she could read my mind, I tried to hide what I was thinking. I wondered if she could see the sinful dream I'd had about Shai that morning. The memory made me blush despite myself.

"Sin is non-existent, it is a man-made condition. It is an attempt by the conquerors to control people. The word comes from archery and means 'missing the mark.' But, as in all things missed, the archer would simply take another arrow and try again."

"You're telling me there is no such thing as sin?"

"Only by virtue of the polarity. Only by comparing it to the good." Sophia shrugged in the innocent way that children did.

"What about Hell?"

"Ha, a long-forgotten truth." She chuckled, her fingers making waves into the air around her for dramatic effect. "*Sheol*, interpreted as Hell or Hades, was, in actuality, a constantly burning dump outside of Jerusalem. It is where the ancient cultures eliminated their refuse."

I laughed at the absurdity of it all. "All this time, how did they convince people to believe in Hell and in sin? How didn't people realize?"

"It is understandable that the world would doubt what they knew to be true. It is what history has taught you to do. It's your ego's way of protecting you from knowledge of that which you seek. But the ego can only hold the barrier up for so long. Eventually, the light of the truth will start to fray at the cloth of the curtain, at the bricks of the wall. Eventually, even doubt and skepticism will give way to curiosity and the pursuit of knowledge. For truth will always tip the scales. Light will always eradicate darkness. Your heart will always hold the greater truth. Energy will always be higher than apathy. All you need is a spark of interest and the whole universe will be shown to you. Would you like that? Would you like to receive this 'instructions manual,' as you called it?"

"I don't really know. I'm not very religious." I let my gaze wander, avoiding direct eye contact, because I was conflicted. *Is that what I wanted?*

"I'm not talking about religion, my little bird. There is no religion higher than truth. Your conflict is your ego's voice, which is based in fear, trying to line up with what you know."

"And religion has nothing to do with it?" I checked.

"It is the Divine Paradox; the collisions of the ego's journey make way for the soul's journey," she continued. "You have become enslaved by your egos, your shadow selves."

"Isn't it the opposite? Aren't we under the control of our egos?"

"Many of your teachers will have you believe that, but the truth is, your soul is free, and it can never be contained. It is your ego that has become enslaved, enslaved to the conditions of your environment. Because the soul has greater awareness, it is up to the soul to embrace the ego. The more the soul nurtures the ego, giving it reassurance, encouragement and enrichment, the more the ego can trust the soul. Then the ego will not resist the soul in its evolution and transformation. It is not a competition between ego and soul, but a collaboration, each side participating in the ultimate goal of the soul's growth. The ego is nothing but your soul's servant, and it's the biggest ally in your quest to achieve your greatest potential."

"So the ego is good?" I asked, shocked to hear this viewpoint. I had been indoctrinated in a world that said that ego meant arrogance, or that a person who had a big ego was only looking out for themselves. It was strange to hear another interpretation. But then again, everything about this woman was strange. In fact, everything about this whole journey was strange. I was beginning to suspect that it might be just me. Maybe I was the strange one.

Sophia shook her head from side to side, making little tsk, tsk, tsk sounds with her tongue. "The ego is neither good nor bad. The ego's nature is simply to return to what it knows, while the soul's nature is to dive into its new potential. The ego has a single agenda—survival. By emancipating your ego, you release yourself from the bondage of knowledge and become an advocate for wisdom."

"I don't think my ego has such control over me..." I started to say, but stopped myself, realizing the hypocrisy.

"It's not just your personal ego that must be emancipated. It is the planetary ego. It's not just the spiritual force that your world must realize, it must also release the material force. The combination of the two is a powerful recipe."

"So, how do we break those shackles? How do we release the ego?"

"You must invite your ego to meet you, as if for the first time. Be curious, gentle, compassionate, for your ego has protected you from harm for many, many years. Now ask it, 'Are you ready to serve the soul?' Then invite it back to you. Invite its strength and talents to serve your soul. Once enough people in your civilization do this, then a shift in your evolution will occur. The Great Turning."

"What is the Great Turning? How does that work?" I suddenly made the connection between what Sophia was saying to what Natalie had said.

"The world has done much to keep people in line with what they know, with what is comfortable. That is the ego. The voice of knowledge, it keeps you from true wisdom. It was not always this way."

"Yeah, probably before religion came along and ruined it all..."

Sophia gave a quintessentially childish laugh, accompanied by a shoulder shrug. "Religion is a man-made invention. Many people before you challenged the dogmas of religion, sometimes to great personal peril. Do you know where this word religion comes from?"

I shook my head no.

"It comes from the Latin word *religio*, which means '*to rebind*.' So, tell me, what is it that became unbound?"

"I don't really know."

"Before religion, there was a fabric that we were all bound to. Each person was a thread of the fabric that made up the universe. Each was the mysterious fiber that connected the whole. But the conquerors shredded the cloth, unfurled the weave and raised the veil of doubt. Many people through the years searched for the truth. They tried to lift the veil. They left the comfort of their beliefs to search and expand what they knew to be true. It starts only with a spark of interest. Once ignited, that spark can become a raging fire, or a flickering candle, but the curiosity must be present. In order to receive it, you must have a desire. A desire for wisdom is the first of all creations. Would you like to learn, little bird? Would you like to expand what you know? Would you like to go on a journey? Are you curious to learn the wisdom of the ages?"

I thought about all that had brought me to this Jerusalem apartment. I thought about all the coincidences and synchronicities along the way. I thought that I had nothing to lose.

I was curious.

And I was scared to leave.

CHAPTER 11

Thursday morning, September 29th
Tel Aviv

The bus ride to the main terminal was longer than I'd expected. There was standing room only, and I missed my stop by a couple of miles. The map I held in front of me was a jumble of streets, crisscrossing and intersecting at impossible angles. The sun peaked through the buildings and the traffic on the roads was already heavy. Though it was early, the heat was already irrepressible. My backpack was heavy, and I could feel a large, wet sweat stain spreading under its weight.

The high-rise towers of the main street gave way to three and four storied stucco buildings. The sand-colored edifices were stained from years of rain and highway soot. Laundry, hung on wire lines outside of windows, told the story of the daily lives of the inhabitants. In one apartment lived a young family, their towels and colorful bathing suits drying in the sun after a day at the beach. Another apartment displayed the olive-green fatigues of a soldier, hanging beside a pair of blue jeans, washed by a mother, happy to have her child come home. Another window's laundry line exhibited the large, white underpants of an old man, beside the large crème bra worn by an old woman. The hanging laundry was a parade of life.

The blue, cloudless sky was vast, providing no shelter from the bright, unrelenting sun. The stone walls, enclosing the perimeter of the buildings, acted as sentries against the explosion of bougainvillea in a deluge of vibrant color—purple, pink, crimson and all shades in between—that threatened to take over the sidewalks. An aroma of sweetness wafted in the air. Between the fence openings, the long stems of red hibiscus flowers would reach for my shoulder, dying my t-shirt with their bright orange powder. The tree branches bowed down, fatigued from clutching the excess weight of the oranges, discarding the over-ripe fruit to the floor. Walking along the sidewalk became an obstacle course, fruit from below, boughs from above, and hibiscus stems from the side.

By the time I reached the imposing white structure of the bus terminal, I was hot and bothered, damp from heat and ready to collapse. The lady behind the glass of the information desk was unhelpful and sardonic when I asked about the schedule for the Jerusalem-bound bus. She sneered before pointing to platform twelve with her pen without even looking up from her Sudoku.

The red dots of the electronic sign indicated that a bus to Jerusalem left on the hour. But at ten minutes past the hour, I ran onto platform twelve and watched the bus pull out of the station without me. Tentatively, I approached the information desk again and asked the lady when the next bus was. She peered up, shrugged her shoulders and returned to her Sudoku. The glass partition that separated us was thick so maybe she couldn't hear me. I tried again, much louder this time. The info lady outright ignored me.

"Why do you not take a Sherut?" a soft, accented voice behind me asked.

Turning quickly, my eyes met a white shrouded figure. In my instantaneous perception, I thought it was a ghost. Or maybe, someone dressed like one. An audible gasp escaped the back of my throat. I caught my breath, then apologetically smiled in an acknowledgement that said, '*I gasped because I didn't know you were there, not because you're wearing a headscarf.*' Yet, I knew that wasn't entirely true.

She smiled back.

"What's a Sherut?" I asked.

"It is like a bus, but also like a taxi. I have also missed the bus, so I am going to take the Sherut. I will show you."

I followed her down the escalators and out into the street. On the way, she casually explained that the Sherut service is a privately owned van, like a taxi, but it drove on the same routing as a bus. It accommodated ten passengers, only leaving the station when it was full. To me, it sounded ingenious.

I took the window spot in the last row, and she sat in the last row also, at the other window. We were the first passengers in the van, and as we waited for eight more, we sat silently. When I looked at her again, I noticed that she was young, about my age. Under her white headscarf, she was dressed a lot like me: long t-shirt, blue jeans, white runners. She had a backpack sitting at her feet just like mine was. She was quite pretty with her olive complexion, big smile, and dancing almond eyes.

She grinned at me, and I awkwardly looked away. Another passenger boarded and sat up front. I opened Natalie's book and began reading.

> *Goddess worship was not a religion of theology, but one of poetry. It was passed on orally as myths, legends, or teachings, to be used as metaphors for every stage of birth, life, death, and rebirth.*
>
> *Goddess symbolism was not a parallel structure to God as Father-Head. Goddess did not rule the world; she was the world. She was not transcendent, living outside of humanity, but immanent, able to internally manifest in each individual. In Mother Goddess, there was nothing to be feared, nothing to be obeyed. No reverence was paid to an angry, wrathful, vengeful, omnipotent, unknowable God.*
>
> *Goddess culture was distinctly earth-based, linking all aspects of nature to the universe.*
>
> *The Goddess represented a journey inward, to the self, to the diversity of existence, and to the beauty in the world.*

"Are you English?" she asked in perfectly practiced intonation, nodding her chin to the book in my hands.

I looked down at the book, unexpectedly embarrassed by its title. I turned it casually in my hands, so the back faced her.

"Yes, I speak English," I answered.

"Oh, good!" Her eyes lit up. "I am hoping to improve my English. Can I practice with you?" she asked with a twinkle.

"I, sure, I guess so," I stammered.

"I am trying to speak as much English as I can. I watch many American movies, read many English books. But speaking, it is very difficult," she said.

"Your English is very good."

She beamed. "Thank you. You think so? I have been studying a long time. It is hard. I study at the university, but then I go home and have no one to practice with."

"No, it's really very good," I repeated.

Two more passengers got on. They were an older couple, indicating by their gestures that they wanted to sit in the two adjacent seats of the back row. The girl with the scarf moved to the seat beside me to let them sit together.

"What do you study at university? What's your major?" I asked.

"I study to be a teacher. That is what good girls in my village do." She smiled at me, a smile that reminded me, rather uncannily actually, of my roommate Beth. "Are you a student also?"

"Yeah, I'm studying anthropology."

"Oh, I like that. It is so interesting. Anthropology, like archaeology. I think it is a very fascinating topic."

"Why don't you just switch to study it then?"

She shook her head. "No, no. I could not do that. No future in that."

"Well, if you love it, then you can pursue it further, go into academia, write, do research, field work. You can do whatever you want to do."

She smiled at me, shrugging her shoulders. "Maybe where you come from girls can do all those things. But in my world, that is not possible. I study something that has a future. Something that will bring a good job. Then I can have good husband."

"What happens then?"

"Then I have good children." She laughed.

I tried to contain my dismay, tried to remain politically correct, but it was hard. "Well, I mean, after you have children? Will you study what you want then?"

She smiled at me again, in that smile that could be Beth. "It is different for me in my world. You have freedoms, you can study what you want, learn what you want, be what you want, get married, not be married, have children, have no children. I have people expecting certain things from me. My family, they expect me to help, to live modestly, to marry and have children, to be part of the community. I cannot just choose whatever I want to study. I am already challenging my family by studying. My *sitte,* my father's mother, insisted that I have an education. So I must study something useful. I cannot study whatever I like, especially not archaeology or anthropology."

I squinted at her. "Why not?"

"It is forbidden."

"Why?"

She looked at me incredulously. "Well, let us say there are the *djinn* that forbid that sort of thing."

"How do you mean?"

She brought her voice to a hushed whisper. "There is an evil spell, a *pulsa dinura,* cast on anyone who disturbs ancient antiquities." She rubbed the amulet on her necklace. It was a small symbol of a hand with a blue eye in the center.

"What are these *djinn*? What do they do?"

"Only bad things befall those who seek to uncover the past. Have you ever heard of the scrolls found at Nag Hammadi?"

I felt my whole body flush, reminded of my time with Shai. Instinctually, I found myself fascinated by the funny coincidence, but then I remembered what Natalie had said about synchronicities.

"Funny, I've heard a little bit about those scrolls lately." I tried to suppress my blush, but I felt my face reddening despite myself.

She didn't seem to notice. "You see, those scrolls were cursed by the *djinn*. Only bad things happen when you look into the past. Two brothers found those scrolls in the desert, their mother tried so much to ruin those scrolls, but the boys defied her. Only tragedy befell them. The *djinn* are very powerful." She kept rubbing at her amulet.

"Do you believe that?"

She giggled then, her eyes sparkling. "I do not know, but you see, I cannot go to study such a thing. My family will forbid it."

A few more passengers trickled on until all of the seats were taken. The driver got on last and took the payment.

"I am Hanan," she introduced herself once the van pulled out of the station.

"I'm Selena."

"Why are you going to Jerusalem? Going to the Old City? Seeing the sights?"

I smiled to myself. I felt odd telling her about Natalie's challenge, or about the cryptic message on the side of a mosque, or about the little bird that seemed to follow me. After Shai had teased me the night before about the Jerusalem Syndrome, I was embarrassed to admit that I was on a mission to find something, or someone, that I knew so little about.

"What do you suggest I do in Jerusalem?"

"Well, of course, you must see *Haram al-Sharif*, the grounds of the *al-Aksa* mosque. It is the most famous sight in *al-Quds*, the famous golden dome. It is a very holy, very special place."

"What is it that makes it so special?"

"It is the *Qubbat al-Sakhra*, the Dome of the Rock. The rock, it is the place where Mohammed took his last step before sending... is that the word in English?" She gestured with both hands upwards.

"Ascending, going up."

"Yes, ascending into heaven."

"Can you tell me that story?" I asked, getting my notebook and pen out.

"Do you like stories?"

"Yes," I laughed. "I love stories. That's why I chose to study anthropology. I call it research," I explained.

"Okay, I will tell you the story, for your research," she agreed good naturedly. "One night, while the Prophet Mohammed was sleeping in his bed, he was awakened by the angel Gabriel. By a miracle, Mohammed could fly, and so made his *isra'*, his Night Journey to what we call *al-Quds*, what you call Jerusalem. There he was greeted by all the great prophets who came before him:

Adam, Abraham, Moses, Aaron, Enoch, John, Joseph and Jesus. They gave him his final teachings before his *mi'raj,* his ascent into the seven Heavens and to the throne of God, then Mohammed surrendered to the Divine Presence."

"That's a beautiful story."

She nodded. "Yes. Mohammed's footprint, as he stepped down into the earth, can still be traced in the Rock."

"I didn't know that," I told her.

"It is also the place where Ibrahim offered his son Ishmael as a sacrifice."

"Didn't Abraham sacrifice Isaac?" I asked, puzzled. I didn't remember much about the Bible, but some stories are more pervasive than others.

Her gaze was gentle, like the endearing look of a mother at her child. She chose her words carefully before continuing. "That is the way the Jews and Christians perceive the story. In Islam, we believe that Ishmael, the firstborn, was the one who Allah wanted sacrificed. When Allah saw that Ibrahim was willing to do it, he accepted the symbol of sacrifice instead. That took place on Mount Moriah, on the rock which is now covered by the Dome of the Rock."

"So is that misunderstanding the real reason for all the centuries of fighting?"

"Who can know the real reason for all the fighting?" She shrugged. "There is a story that tells that when the Prophet was asked 'What is religion?' he answered, 'Religion is the way we conduct ourselves toward others.' In Arabic we say, *salaam aleikum*, peace be upon you. We can only hope that it will one day be true. *Salaam* in the world."

We sat silently, looking out the window. I thought about what she'd said. How funny that just that morning, I had contemplated the elusive nature of peace.

We were driving out of the city, on the highway passing the Ben-Gurion airport. The tail fins of the parked airplanes were like motionless flags. Lufthansa, Air France, Delta, Air Canada, KLM, Swissair, SAS, El Al, Air India. The birds of the world resting in one nest.

As the van sped by the perimeter of the airport, a small figure caught my sight. The *bulbul* sat, perched on top of the barbed-wire fence, impervious to the hazards.

What was it about that bird? Was it really following me? Or was I just noticing it more often than I normally would and then attaching my own significance to it? Was the bird giving me a riddle to solve, or was I making a riddle and looking to the bird for a clue? Either way, I felt impelled towards it. Like those pictures I used to enjoy looking at when I was a kid, the ones that if I stared at long enough and squinted my eyes in just the right way, a different picture would materialize. As a kid, I realized that the whole time that I focused on trying to figure out what was in the picture, it would remain elusive. It was in the moment that I softened my eyes, almost giving up on seeing, that the picture of the dolphin or the tree would materialize. And once I saw it, it seemed as plain as day, as obvious as if it were there the whole time. What were those called again? Holographs? 3-D Kaleidoscopes? Optical illusions?

The *bulbul* held the same attraction as those cryptic pictures for me. I felt that if I could just see it in a different way, it would make sense. I would see the hidden picture. I would understand the bigger message.

"Is this book about anthropology?" Hanan asked, bringing me back into reality.

Natalie's book still sat in my lap. I turned the book and showed her the front cover. "Yes it is. Actually, I met the author on my flight here."

Her eyes grew large and curious. "Really? The author! Was he coming here?"

"Well, actually, *she*, and yes she was. In fact, she is the reason I'm going to Jerusalem."

"Are you meeting her there? How exciting!"

"Um, no, I mean, I don't know. She mentioned something to me and told me she was going to search for it, or for her, rather. But I didn't make any plans to meet her. I hope I can find her, though."

"What do you mean? Search for who?"

I hesitated. I was reticent to admit it to Hanan. She seemed reasonable, logical, sane—all the things I normally considered myself to be. Yet, here I was chasing down this enigma, this rumor, this dream. It sounded too weird.

I shook my head, dismissing her question.

"Are you searching for the author? Or for someone else?" she persisted.

"Not me. The author, Natalie. She mentioned that she was searching for someone, a woman. A wise woman. Someone called a Nevea."

"Ahh, the *Nebea*..." She nodded her head in comprehension. "Yes! Have you heard of her?"

Hanan smiled in amusement. "It is an old, ancient story that the women of my culture would tell. Every few years the story returns, and women from all over the world come to *al-Quds* to find her. So, your friend, this author, must be searching for her, yes?"

"Yes, yes. Exactly. What is the story? Who is this Nevea?"

Hanan looked at me. "Selena, that is a long and complicated story, one that I don't think you would quite understand."

I leaned towards her and almost inaudibly whispered, "I could try."

She smiled and shrugged her shoulders in the same way that Beth would. Their resemblance was eerily striking. It was weird.

She shook her head. "It is too dangerous. The *djinn* would be tempted." She rubbed the pendant on her necklace again. "It is best left to the lips of old women and the ears of young girls. It is best to leave it as an old woman's story, a secret."

"Hanan, I would really like to know this story. I mean, for my research assignment." I could tell that her mind was made up, so I tried a different approach—the truth. "Hanan, I don't know how to explain it, but I feel that ever since I met Natalie, I've been getting these signs. I can't help but feel that I must go searching for the Nevea. There is this little bird that seems to follow me, and yesterday I saw this graffiti that said the words *know peace*. And somehow, I know it doesn't make any sense, but somehow, I feel that I must find her. It's as if I'm on a journey and I must get to the end..." I was rambling. "Please, tell me about the Nevea."

Hanan did not answer me.

Outside, the landscape swished by. The highway gave way to an undulating road. There were towns dotting the hills on either side of the road, homes built in varying heights into the foundation of the hills. The tall towers of the minarets anchored into the center of the towns stood like beacons, lonely structures amidst the sea of brick. In the field next to the road were a few old, rusting tanks, remnants of some bygone war, a glaring reminder of the history of the land. Like a piece of art displayed on a mantle, left there by the previous owner. But unlike art, these antiquities were left to decompose and wither. Exposed to the elements, these tanks were mere shells of what they were built for, recognizable only by a people who knew their purpose. Now, they lay in this makeshift roadside graveyard, a glaring reminder of Mother Nature's attempt to slowly reclaim even the tools of war. But, the sad reality is that even as these relics of war die in waste, newer, stronger, and more effective tools of annihilation are being built.

My ears popped as the bus climbed and descended along the road. I opened and closed my mouth to relieve the pressure.

"My grandmother, my *sitte*, spoke of her when I was young." Hanan's words brought me out of my daydream. "She said there would be a day when she returned to teach us, to guide us." She was staring at the headrest of the seat in front of her, speaking more to herself than to me. "I thought it was the strange, crazy talk of an old woman. But I loved to hear her stories. Her stories were so different from what I learned in school, so I knew I was not allowed to tell her stories to anyone. But, I thought they were stories, fictions, fantasies…but then when I saw the name of the book…that is exactly what my *sitte* used to say…the return of the goddess…" Her voice trailed off as if to consider what to say next.

After a moment, she turned to look at me. "Okay, I will tell you what my *sitte* said, because you asked me, and—I can't explain why—but I think my *sitte* wants me to tell you, Allah have mercy." She took a deep breath before continuing. "Where do I begin? Do you know about the Qu'ran?" She waited to see me nod my head before continuing in a rushed whisper. "Well, there are *Suras* in the Qu'ran that we do not study, that we do not read, and that we do not talk about. The scholars forbid it. They explained that the *Suras*, the verses, are not the work of Mohammed, but the work of Satan, the Satanic Verses. These *Suras* tell of the daughters of Allah: Al-Lat, the Goddess of the moon, Al-Uzza, the Goddess of the North Star, and Manat, the Goddess of destiny. The verses say that these Goddesses are the birds, the messengers who we have been waiting and hoping for. My *sitte* used to tell me that when the Goddesses return, they would bring with them peace and happiness in the world. She used to pray for the Goddesses to come and release this world from evil. She said when they returned, they would bring us signs. She told me I must watch for the signs, but she never told me what they were. I wish she would have told me what to look for."

Hanan stopped speaking for a few moments. She took a corner of her headdress and wiped a tear that was forming. She took a deep breath, held it in and then slowly exhaled. "My *sitte* died last month, *Allah yerhamah,* may Allah be with her soul."

"I'm sorry, Hanan."

She nodded, her *hijab* dabbing away fresh tears.

"I know how you feel. My mom died in May."

"Oh, Selena, I am so sorry."

"It's okay, Hanan. Thank you." I said, grateful for this strange new friendship.

We sat silently together for the rest of the ride into Jerusalem. Hanan continued to weep gently into her headscarf, and I found myself doing something I had never done in public. I cried. In all the months of sitting at my mother's bedside, the years of being on my own, the days when the loneliness and despair threatened to turn me inside out, I had never cried. Even at the funeral, I refused to let my tears escape. Only the nights were left unguarded, when the pillow would muffle my sobs and the darkness would swallow up my anguish. But, with Hanan mourning the death of her *sitte* so candidly, I caught the fever of her sadness. We wept openly and mutually.

The tears ran silently down my cheeks and fell into my lap. After so many years of being repressed, they poured out of me like a rushing river, eroding the dams I had worked so hard to build. At first, I wept for Hanan, at least that's what I tried to convince myself. Then, without my consent, my tears found freedom and they reveled in it. I began to cry for all the hurt of my childhood, all the pain I had been carrying, all the doubts and fears and inequities of my life. And then I cried for my mother, and my love for her and her love for me. Eventually, quickly as they came, my tears left me.

We were the last passengers to pile out of the van. We stood on the street for a long time, postponing our goodbye. Finally,

Hanan broke the silence. "Thank you, Selena. You have given me much comfort. Thank you for listening. I wish there was more I could tell you."

"No, no, Hanan. I should be the one thanking you. Thank you for sharing your story with me." I reached into my backpack and handed her Natalie's book. "Here, I want you to have this. Something to remember me by." I smiled and held it forward.

Her hands came up in front of her, palms towards me. "No, I cannot take your book. Thank you, but I cannot."

"Consider it one of *sitte*'s signs," I insisted. Her hands stopped protesting, and she accepted *The Return of the Goddess*. She opened her backpack to put it in and pulled out a long white scarf, a headdress just like the one she was wearing.

"Then I will give you this." She handed it to me. "It will keep you safe, protect you on your journey to find the *Nebea*."

I was about to protest, then realized that would be hypocritical, so I took the scarf and put it in my backpack. "Thank you, Hanan. I hope we can meet again."

"I hope so too, Selena."

We stood awkwardly for a long time; the space between us filled with many words left unsaid. Finally, she slung her backpack on her shoulders.

"*Ma'a salame,* go in peace, Selena," she called out to me as she walked out of the station and into the Jerusalem streets.

CHAPTER 12

Thursday night, September 29ᵗʰ
Old City of Jerusalem

The moon radiated through the open window. The calamity outside seemed to have died down, and I considered trying to get back to Tel Aviv. Would I even find my way out of Jerusalem in the dark? Would there be taxis? Would I be safe?

I must have been lost in thought because, without noticing how it got there, on the makeshift table in front of me sat a brass platter with plates of hummus, warm pita bread, tomatoes and wine. I was suddenly famished because I hadn't eaten since breakfast.

"Eat, eat, little bird, and I shall tell you of the parable of the little swallow in the forest."

I ripped a corner of the bread and dug in. I finished half of the hummus and took a few long sips of wine before she spoke again. When she did, I slowed my chewing to listen.

"There was once a great flood in the forest," she started. "All of the animals, sensing what was coming, fled to higher ground. All but one little swallow who flew towards the direction of the flood. He passed by the wise old owl, who assumed the swallow was confused and tried to help him to safety. But, the swallow replied that he was returning to the forest to see if anyone needed his help. The owl tried to reason with him, but seeing that his mind was made up, the owl acquiesced and continued on his way. When the swift and nimble mockingbird overheard the swallow's ambitions, she ridiculed him. 'How could something so small and fragile help anything else?' she laughed. But, the swallow would not be deterred and continued on his way. When the swallow passed the vulture, the vulture mocked him. 'What benefit will you gain?' asked the vulture, who himself was anticipating the spoils of the storm. But, the swallow would not be dissuaded. He continued into the forest until he found a baby hummingbird deep in water, flailing its wings, about to drown. He swooped down and saved the baby and flew her to safety. When she asked why he had endangered his own life to save her, the swallow responded simply, 'Wings are useless unless they help others fly.'"

I had devoured the plate of hummus and most of the tomatoes. I turned the wine glass in my hand, allowing myself to languish with each sip and with the story.

"I suppose that story has something to do with the next sacred sphere? Let me guess, something about helping others?"

"Not quite, little bird. This sphere is of rhythm. Everything that exists does so in rhythm. Everything flows, out and in, everything has its own tides, ebbs and flows. The pendulum swing manifests in everything. This is a universal law, in suns, moons, worlds, mind, energy and matter. The great alchemists knew that the magic lies in using rhythm instead of being used by rhythm. It is simply an awareness to align with your intentions. It means that in every act, you must choose whether you will be logical like the owl, whether you will be proud like the mockingbird, or will you choose your own self-interest like the vulture. Or, like the swallow, will you pursue your intentions? Even at the cost of ridicule? Or personal jeopardy? Even if it is not sensible to do so?"

"Okay, but, the swallow didn't *intend* to save the baby bird. He just thought of doing the right thing, and then he *happened* to find the baby to save. It could have gone differently; he could have found nothing to save, or he could have died."

"Each time you make a choice in your life, you change your awareness, the path of your consciousness. Your consciousness literally changes frequencies as a response to your choices. The energy of your intention re-creates itself over and over again as it travels, getting stronger and stronger, until, ultimately, a solid reality is formed. The messages sent by your intentions create a harmonized relationship with the universe. That relationship becomes your new reality. The key to creating a new reality is to focus on the outcome rather than the process."

I stretched my arms above my head. Feeling tired and satiated from a full belly, I nestled into the sofa. "So, all I need to do is set my intention about something? How is that supposed to work?" I asked, thinking of the time my mother spent in the hospital, sure that my mother had no intention to be there.

"When you set your intention, creation responds by bringing that to you. The word *kivun*, direction, has the same root as the word *kavannah*, intention. Your intentions create your experience. Whether you have positive or negative intentions, your thoughts are reverberations of that energy. When you focus your attention on something, you are, essentially, making a decision on what you desire to occur. You are creating a channel for the realization of that new reality to become manifest."

"Well, what about someone who is sick…let's say someone has cancer. Does that mean their intention is to die?"

"It simply means that the intention of their life had its focus elsewhere."

Her answer made me stop and think. I had never thought of it in that way. I always thought that cancer had just happened to my mom, refusing to believe the pop-psychology that she had somehow willed it onto herself. While she was sick, people kept telling her to will her sickness away, to believe that it would go and that the cancer cells would somehow listen. I'd never understood that line of thinking. It was as if by willing them away, she could somehow prevent herself from dying, but when that didn't happen, the onus of responsibility for her disease fell on her shoulders. As if she hadn't "thought the cancer away" enough. I'd always considered that advice to be a bunch of nonsense. But, now, Sophia was suggesting it from a different angle. It wasn't that my mom didn't "think away" her cancer enough; it was that her main intention in her life was my survival. And at that, she succeeded, even though she died.

It made me wonder what I was focused on in my life. Work, school, ensuring I didn't make the same mistake my mom did, ending up pregnant and alone. By default, I had adopted the strategy of my mother's intention for me: survival. I rarely gave any thought to what my soul wanted or what made me feel alive.

"How is my intention different than my essence?" I asked.

"If you live your life with intention, then your purpose, your soul's essence will find you. In Hebrew, the two words, direction and intention, are related at their root letters. When you set your direction, *kivun*, and align it with your intention, *kavannah*, you awaken to your purpose, your essence. This is how you create conscious reality. It is as if you are weaving a garment of your spirit and power into the web of your entire existence. It is thus that you may become a positive force, where opulence and harmony are attracted to you. When you are awake enough to start asking questions, it is an indication that your soul is prodding you to return to your intentions. Thoughts about your essence are really your essence trying to reconnect with you. There is a silent something within you that intends to express itself. That something is your soul. Listen."

I turned the wine glass in my hands. There seemed to be so much in my life that happened without my intending it to— school, work, my mom getting sick. Even the last couple of days seemed like they were happening to me, without my intention and without my control.

As if reading my thoughts, Sophia said, "To be in harmony with whatever it is you intend to create becomes the symphony which is responsible for all of creation. *Become* the intention and you will become one with the universal creator. You will transcend the ego-mind and unify with the universal mind."

The wine was having a numbing effect on *my* mind. Sophia's words were slowing my thoughts. I tried to process everything that she was saying, but it was futile.

"Do you remember the story of Lilith, the wife of Adam?" she asked as she gently put her glass on the platter. She placed her hands, palms together, on her lap. "Such a beautiful story, an inspiring secret. The men who wrote the history books portrayed her without the glory of truth. The Story Women passed down a different legend."

I was confused. "Isn't Adam from the Bible? Wasn't Eve his wife? Are you saying the Bible is a history book? And I thought you didn't want to talk about religion?" I asked, still resistant.

"Ahh, my little bird, you are right. It is said that the Bible is Black Fire on White Fire. That the black ink with which it is written can only be understood with the secret knowledge of white stories that were passed on from mother to daughter, sister to sister, woman to woman. The Black is what the men wrote, the White is what the women told. I care not about the Black Fire stories by themselves. Black Fire has created what is happening on the streets of this city and of others. Black Fire has brought war and anger. Black Fire has separated and divided. Black Fire has burned and destroyed, ravaged and raped, killed and crucified. Sing not the song of Black Fire. Sing to me only in the language of White Fire. Sing to me of beauty and grace, wisdom and strength, glory and splendor. Sing only songs of unity. Speak only words of peace. And if those words elude you, then find solace in the silence."

I breathed deeply, absorbing her words. Sophia's voice was hypnotic. I drank some more wine and allowed it to dim the sharp edges of my fears.

We sat in comfortable silence for many minutes before she quietly continued. "The Black stories have been interpreted and contorted to suppress the masses, to keep them ignorant of the true purpose and direction of their lives. The religious interpretations are not, and were never meant to be, the true nature of reality. They hold a clue to a much bigger understanding. An understanding that, up until now, would have been too much for humanity to take in. So, the stories were explained as just that: stories, parables with a moral code, directives for a civilized existence, in short, religion. And then the tragedy began, and these beautiful words were used against people. Words, misinterpreted and held over them to make them feel shame and guilt, sin and repentance, all notions that religion espoused but were never part of the original plan. Over the years, there were scholars who learned the true meaning. They gained an understanding beyond the parable. Those were the enlightened, the mystics, the wise. Unfortunately, those brave and truthful souls were usually condemned by their fellow men."

It was true, I thought, as I pondered the lives of some of my heroes, Gandhi, Martin Luther King Jr., Joan of Arc. Humans kept destroying all the people who fought to make positive change. I took a swig from my glass and put my chin in my hands.

"So, what is the story of Lilith?"

"The story of Lilith is encoded into Genesis. She was first wife of Adam, who lived with him in the Garden of Eden, in Paradise."

"Are you saying that Paradise was a real place? Not just a metaphor?"

"My little bird, there are many levels of interpretation, written in code. In ancient languages there are no vowels and what's left are the letters that make the acronym P.R.D.S.—Paradise. The first level of interpretation is Parable. If any story is told as just a story, it has the charm and wisdom of a great tale. If anyone wants to stop there, then that is where they should stop, because they are not ready for more. A tale also teaches us lessons about life and morality that exists at the level of Rules. Awareness of the moral of the story is always a helpful guidance to people. They base the way they live, their traditions, and their culture on their interpretation of those morals. Peel the layers further and you find a Dilemma, a riddle in the letters that reveals a code. And further still is a Secret. It is this secret that is the jewel. It is the secret that is the pearl, the elusive crown of all knowledge."

"Does the story of Lilith contain a secret?" I wondered out loud, curious about this mystery.

Sophia smiled. "The Story Women slipped secrets into all of the stories. They are the ancient archetypes of every woman who has ever existed. They are the creators of the feminine energy. They reveal the truth about our roles in the universe, as well as our knowledge of it."

"And the Story Women passed down the stories?" I thought of the myth of the Simorgh that the crew-bus driver had shared, and of Hanan's *sitte*'s goddess stories.

"The stories and their true meanings have always lived through the mouths of the Story Women. We would gather together and tell the stories. We would dance the stories for each other, and the stories would come alive. We would beat the rhythm and our gestures would expose all the secrets. We would paint the riddles onto our hands and onto our feet, the enigma of the patterns. We would sing the songs of mystery as we gathered to fill our water at the wells. Mothers would pass the knowledge down to their daughters, aunts to nieces, nursemaids to infants, mistresses to handmaids. We would ululate the stories in our tents, whisper them in the bath-houses, and reveal them at weddings, births and deaths. We would gather with neighboring women to trade gifts, herbs and medicines, but more than that, we would trade our stories. When a midwife went to a neighboring town, she would take the stories with her, and she would return with stories. The children would be weaned with the stories, would play amidst the stories, would understand the stories and carry them on. That is how they stayed alive.

Unfortunately, in our history, these stories have been interpreted from a patriarchal viewpoint. The stories of the Goddesses have been skewed to make women subordinate to men, lesser than men. This has taken away the power that was rightfully and originally ours. The time has come for us to reclaim that power, to hold our position beside the masculine, to find our inner feminine once more. Only when we do that can we release the bonds of patriarchy that have held us down for so long. The time has come, little bird."

"Why now?" I asked.

"All the prophets and sages, from cultures and societies as varied as there are people, have pointed to this time. This is a critical point of our evolution. The balance between the masculine and feminine energies must be restored if we are going to continue to thrive. The planet, the politics, the state of disharmony we feel in all aspects of our lives must come to equilibrium. The secret of the Goddess will soon be found and revealed."

"Are you a Story Woman?" I asked.

"I am." She peered at me over her teacup. "As are you, my little bird. As was your mother, as was her mother before her."

The air in the room was potent. I took in what Sophia was saying, about my mother being a Story Woman. I thought of how many stories I missed hearing her tell. I imagined her alive and well, telling me the stories that were told to her. I imagined living in a different time, a time when women would gather and listen to the stories that the Story Women would tell, just like I was doing. In my mind, I heard the laughter of children, the solace of women, and their soft whispers. I imagined that the room I was in was full of beautiful, numinous women, all sitting on cushions as I was. I saw the divan, and the Story Woman revealing the secrets. But in my reverie, the woman sitting on the divan was not Sophia. It was me.

"So now I'm curious. What is the secret story of Lilith?"

"Ah, my little bird, you have such curiosity. Your mind is sharp; you love questions. This is good. Questions are the fuel of the soul. Always question and always look for truth. The word question comes from the word *questio*, Latin for 'to seek.' In English, you use the word quest. We must always be on a quest. This is the only way to expand, to keep the flames of knowledge alight."

The compliment, and the wine, made me blush.

She beamed at me proudly. "Once upon a time, the people of Canaan lived peaceably amongst each other. They worshipped the Goddess, under her many names and many manifestations.

Whatever name was bestowed to her, she always took the form of the three female divine archetypes; the wild maiden, the great mother, and the wise old woman. The Lilith, the Eve and the Shekinah. Lilith was the dark, feminine side. It was Lilith who would not be subservient to Adam, and Lilith who demanded her own autonomy and who controlled the serpent. With Lilith, the wild nature of woman could be released. She awoke the desires and the sensuality, the fire and the ferocity. With her, the serpent was a divine positive figure, not a negative one, the keeper of the secrets of creation and the Universe. The male-God oriented Conquerors rejected the Goddess and repudiated the serpent. Threatened by the power of the wild woman, the Conquerors vilified Lilith and demonized the serpent. But, the Garden of Eden was the serpent's place. The serpent, which sheds its skin and renews life just as the moon sheds its shadow, was the master of the Tree of Knowledge, where eternity and time come together. The serpent was born again, as the moon was born again. The moon and the serpent are equivalent symbols. The symbol of the Goddess as the giver of life, the field that produces all forms."

"Why doesn't anyone teach this? Why don't we all know it?" I asked, thinking of how damaging it has been to our collective psyches to constantly have to hide that part of ourselves that is wild and dark. How freeing it would be not to hide from that part that feels attraction, not to mention lust and longing. Even as I thought of the desires that had threatened to overwhelm me with Shai, I felt released, not embarrassed anymore. I felt freedom within.

"They soon will, darling little bird. They soon will."

CHAPTER 13

Thursday morning, September 29ᵗʰ
Old City of Jerusalem

I entered through the Jaffa Gate into an open expanse cobble-stoned area. The morning sun, already shining a bright orange, peeked above the high stone wall. The city appeared to be illuminated. The stones were the color of sand, speckled with glints of sparkle, the spaces between them aged and grey. Between some of the stones, green moss grew and pigeons somehow nested into cumbersome crevices.

The place was a contradiction. Everywhere I looked, the ancient was juxtaposed against the modern. The streets were made of old, uneven cobble-stones, but the storefronts were neon-lit and up to date. The ramparts towered like an aged bastion, but electrical lines hung like streamers across the open air. There was even what looked to be a Rabbi, rushing by while talking on his cell phone, its antenna poking playfully in his side locks of hair.

More than that, it was much bigger than I thought it would be, but then again, I didn't know what I'd expected. I looked for Natalie or any of her friends. I started to doubt my decision to come here. I felt naïve. Did I really think I could just waltz into

Jerusalem and find her? There were already throngs of people there, mostly tourists congregating in groups, though a few monks in long, brown robes walked purposefully and young men wearing black suits and fur-lined black hats headed in the direction of the inner streets, along with men wearing checkered scarves. It was as if I was in a time warp, taken back a few hundred years, with only the tourists to anchor me in the now.

The tour groups and religious pilgrims, distinct by their matching t-shirts or backpacks, stood in flocks, encircling their tour guides. Each of the obscured guides held a long pole topped with something to differentiate them—a flag, a streamer, a ball. It made me think of a lighthouse, like a beacon for the group to follow through the streets.

I went into the tourist information office for a map, though studying it did nothing to help me figure out which way to go. I decided to follow the orange-shirted Japanese group, with the purple flapping butterfly pole leading the way.

We left the open area and headed into the closed corridor of the street. The low buildings blocked out the sun, creating a cool atmosphere in the stone passageway. The alleyway seemed as wide as my outstretched arms, though as cramped as they were, it was impossible to tell. It was crowded with people and lined with shop-fronts. The forceful vendors approached, with invitations to enter their stores and try their products. Displayed were little trinkets, religious souvenirs, tourist mementos, spices, t-shirts, antiques, glassware, candy, tunics, coin belts, shoes. Anything and everything was sold in that market. I tried to not make eye contact with the pushy merchants, but they were insistent. It seemed that as soon as I managed to get rid of one, another took his place.

"Come lady...I show you nice things..."

"No, thank you." I rushed away, trying to avoid eye contact.

"Come to my store...free...no pay..."

"No, thank you." I picked up my pace as he stepped towards me.

One of the stalls had canvas bags with multi-hued spices, mounds of luscious green, or dazzling red, orange, purple. The name of each spice was written in crude handwriting on cardboard name-tags topping wooden sticks. It looked to me like a spice cemetery. The names of the spices were foreign and exotic sounding, names like *za'atar, bokharat* and *sumac*. The aromatic smells were pungent and intoxicating.

"Allo, where you from, lady? Come, I give good price."

"No, thank you." I was practically running.

The stone steps were awkward to navigate as they led me down, deeper into the abyss. The shopkeepers were menacing; the alleyways, ominous. The walls were closing in on me. I had never done well in tight spaces. I searched desperately for the purple butterfly as I made my way through the crowd. I saw it disappear to the right as I hurried to catch up.

"Pretty lady...you want nice souvenir?"

I made it around the corner and out of the market street. The air cleared and I could breathe again. I followed the group as they headed towards an open area through a security check-point and down the stairs.

We were on the grounds of an open area, an expanse surrounded by stone walls. People milled around the cordoning perimeter, where tourists could take pictures, visitors congregated and sightseers gathered with their guides.

The purple butterfly herded her tour group together to tell them the history of the place. The Japanese translator echoed her explanation while the orange t-shirts huddled around her. I stood a few feet away, listening in and making shorthand notes into my notebook. She told the story of the Temple, originally built by King Solomon, who was given the plans by his father, King David, in approximately 1000 BCE. It was said, she told, to have been built entirely by volunteer craftsmen and stonemasons, every stone extracted from the local quarries and hand-carved to perfectly align with the others. The endeavor to build the great Temple was extraordinary, an effort made even more remarkable by the cooperation of the tribes from far and away. It was demolished in 586 BCE during the Babylonian expulsion. As the purple butterfly explained, many of the treasures from the Temple were either stolen or never found, including what some suspect to be the Ark of the Covenant. Hidden in the inner sanctum of the Temple, the Ark of the Covenant was in the Holy of Holies, the place where only the high priest was allowed to enter, and even he was only allowed once a year.

Then, a few decades later, the Babylonians were defeated by the Persians, who allowed the Second Temple to be rebuilt by Zerubbabel in 515 BCE, though it was not until Herod the Great started rebuilding it in 22 BCE that the grandiose construction started. Herod built the astonishing Temple onto a raised platform, an area the size of twelve football fields and thirty-two meters high, which was supported on all sides by the four massive retaining walls. It was finally finished in 55 CE, by Herod's great-grandson. The wall in front of us, the Western Wall, explained the butterfly, was the only wall remaining after the Roman invasion in 70 CE. This is the place that Jews have gathered for the last two thousand years to mourn the loss of the Temple, which is why it's called the Wailing Wall.

The purple butterfly lady ushered her group closer to the wall, instructing the orange-shirts to write a little note, a divine wish, which they could stuff into the cracks as a direct request to God. I decided to hang back on my own.

Jerusalem was not at all what I had expected. I thought it would be uncluttered and orderly, like a museum. Yet, here I was, amidst a stone city, overwhelming in energy, a cacophony of sights, smells and sounds. I was thankful to be in this open area, where I could breathe the air and not feel trapped. A pang of anxiety struck me. If I were to continue to search for Natalie, or for her friends, or for the Nevea, I would have to go back into those anxiety inducing streets. I considered leaving and started looking for an exit strategy. On my right I could see the tour buses and taxis beyond the outer perimeter of the walled city. Knowing the way out was there calmed me.

In front of me, beyond the roped off areas, men dressed in long black coats and wearing fur lined hats, despite the September heat, swayed violently in prayer towards the wall. On the other side of the partition, in the smaller area to the very right, were the women. I noticed that the women's area, being much smaller than the men's, was much fuller with women in prayer.

I found a spot on the stone steps and opened my notebook to write. As I did, it fell open to the page where I'd glued the second of M's letters, the only one that didn't have an envelope.

I read it again, for the countless time.

> *Ma Chérie Deborah,*
>
> *My mind won't stop thinking of you. Please, please, send word of your well-being. I do not want to imagine you any other way, but, as the days pass, I find myself worrying that you are somehow hurt. My heart longs for you.*
>
> *The situation here remains dire. The post office remains under siege. Possibly your letters are en route. I hope you are receiving mine, though the organization assures me that internal mail has been unencumbered.*
>
> *The fanatics have set up guerrilla training bases along the borders. I plan to visit them tomorrow. I can only hope my presence can bring some much needed peace to the camps.*
>
> *Do you read from the book I gave you?*
>
> *I can only imagine that the words it contains give you the same solace they give me. In the words of the poet;*

Give your hearts, but not into each other's keeping.
For only the hand of Life can contain your hearts.
And stand together, yet not too near together:
For the pillars of the temple stand apart,
And the oak tree and the cypress grow not in each
other's shadow.

I hope you will write soon, my love. I imagine
you are under a beautiful, warm sun, and I imagine
myself with you. It won't be long. I am sure this war
shall end soon.
I cannot wait until I can see you again.

In adoration,

M

P.S. Mon âme te cherchera à tout jamais.

No matter how many times I read that letter, a wave of sympathy for M rushed through me. I wished I knew why my mother didn't write him back. I wished I knew who M was. I wished I knew if he was my father.

I read the words again, surprised by the increased amount of coincidences, or synchronicities. It was weird that of all times, of all places, that my notebook would fall open on this letter, speaking of the pillars of the temple while I was visiting the site of the temple. The goosebumps raised on my arms of their own volition, even though the heat of the sun was pleasantly warming my skin.

I flipped to find a new page, but the words I wrote the day before caught my eye. *Know Peace.* I took a deep breath and contemplated the words. I definitely had not known peace when I was in the market street. I had been scared and critical, the exact opposite of what I promised myself I would be. I re-wrote the words on the corner of another page and ripped that piece of paper out. With that tiny note folded and crumpled in my hand, I made my way into the women's section. The area was humming with voices in private prayer, like the soft buzz of cicadas in a field. Some women were sitting on cheap plastic lawn chairs; some, standing with their prayer books concealing their faces, and some were rocking their sleeping infants back and forth in strollers. I made my way to the very right, found an empty spot and placed the note into the wall.

It seemed unfinished. I wanted to say something, think something, pray something, but I didn't know what. I stood there with my finger on my note for a long time. I looked around, feeling like some weird interloper, disguised as a person who actually felt something while praying. I didn't. Besides, who would I pray to? What would I ask for? My mom was already dead, my father long gone, and I was doing just fine on my own. I had never really asked God for anything, and it seemed too contrived to do it in this place, as if I was saying—"Hey God, funny meeting you here..."

I chuckled louder than I meant to, and a woman beside me looked up from her prayer book and shot me a disapproving look.

I really couldn't think of any prayer words so I did the only thing that seemed right; I silently repeated the words written on my note—*know peace, know peace, know peace, know peace.* I tried to make the words true, but I was being an imposter.

What I really wanted to know was who my father was. From the crevices above me, I heard, *bly, bly, bly.* The *bulbul* was mocking me.

CHAPTER 14

Thursday night, September 29th
Old City of Jerusalem

We sat silently for some time. An involuntary blinking of my eye brought me to the realization that I had been staring at the window without really focusing on it. The breeze wafting in made me aware that the window was slightly open. I wished Sophia would close it. All the chaos outside seemed to have quieted down, which made me feel even more vulnerable.

"Do you know the meaning of the name Adam?" Sophia asked, as if sensing my fear rise.

"No, but I always thought it was strange that the word 'Adam' and the word 'atom' sound the same."

"Yes, they are homonyms." She winked. "Atoms also have masculine and feminine energies that bond to create matter."

I smiled. "I guess it's more than just a coincidence, huh?"

"Much more than mere coincidence—code."

"So what is the Adam, or atom, a code for?"

"There exists, somewhere in the world, a book so old that modern scientists, if they ever found it, would ponder over its pages and argue back and forth forever. They would go mad trying to understand it with their logical minds. From that book came the

Siphra Dzeniouta, a literary relic in and of itself. In it, there is an illustration of Adam as a luminous arc forming a circle and then attaining the highest point possible in the circle's circumference, bending back again, returning to the Earth, ultimately bringing a higher type of humanity in his vortex."

"Wow." I exclaimed, letting all the air out of my lungs, realizing that I had been holding my breath as she spoke. I pictured a spiral, like a tornado, or a whirlwind, twisting and coiling, decimating and destroying. I tried to think of something witty, or at least cogent, to say, but all that I could muster up was another "Wow."

"Wow, indeed. You see 70,000 years ago, humankind was half ethereal in nature. Then, man communed freely with the now unseen universes. Before mystic Adam, many races of beings lived and died out, each less evolved than the next."

"What do you mean by mystic Adam?"

"Adam Kadmon, the mystic Adam that existed before primordial Adam came into being. The names Adam and Eve are merely metaphors for the primordial vessel whose existence came before creation thus encompassing all souls of humanity to come. The name Adam is derived from the word for *adamah*, earth. That means he is made from the very essence of creation. The story tells that primordial Adam received all of the alchemical secrets of Heaven and Earth. An angel greeted primordial Adam at the gates of Eden and instructed him in all the secrets of the spheres. The angel promised that when humankind had mastered the spheres, the ban on the Tree of Knowledge would be lifted and humanity could return to Eden."

I sat cross-legged with my elbows on my knees. "I think I've heard this before…In Genesis, right?"

Sophia nodded. "The story of Genesis holds many codes, yes. The Book of Genesis says '*Thus elohim,*' which literally means Gods and Goddesses, '*created man in his own image male and female, created he them.*' You see, the male and female were one, a unified image. No separation existed between them. But the *elohim* is only one aspect of the origin of the Universe. The *elohim* is the prospect and the possibility. The story of Genesis was a metaphor, a metaphor for the conquerors killing the Goddess culture, a code for the tillers of soil killing the herders, just as in Cain killing Abel."

"So the stories are not just about the beginning of the Universe? You're saying they're kind of like a running commentary of history?"

"Yes, that is right. The beginning, the genesis, of the ever-expanding universe, summed up into metaphor and then the rest is code. In order to understand the future, we must look to the codes of the past. Codes are, of course, riddles not literal interpretations. So the riddle of Adam and Eve is told as such; the creator was light and energy, the infinite and unlimited. The light energy grew and condensed into the form of matter, therefore becoming limited and finite. Atom, Adam, took the form, the primordial matter. From the form of matter came minerals, plants, animals, humans. Because all of creation was light, the instance that the form appeared, a shadow was cast. This shadow was atom's void. The void of the atom filled with more energy, creating energy where only shadow existed. That is why she is called Eve—life. Atoms filled with life energy. Eve *enlivened* the void within the atom, which by itself is void of energy. Adam filled with Eve. They were not a man and woman from our world, but rather the spiritual forces which bestow and receive. In this way, in the act of bestowing and receiving, they ascended to the level of the Creator."

"So, the original sin…"

"Adam and Eve did not sin; they transferred from wholly spiritual forces to material elements. You see Adam and Eve were originally connected, in the image of the creator, yin and yang, Shakti and Shiva, male and female. They were but one body, unified back to back, facing away from each other. They could not see each other, but neither could they see from the same view. When they tasted the fruit of knowledge, they became separate from each other. The instant they became separate, they were confronted with their otherness. In that moment they realized they were naked. From this was born shame of being seen, the fear of losing control. So, they put on their egos as masks to cover them. And then, they saw each other as a reflection of each other for the first time, a reflection of their egos."

"I thought Eve was made from Adam's rib?"

"A code word, *tselah*, the word for her shadow, if mistranslated can mean rib. Yet, just a few verses previous, which reads that man and woman were made in god's *tselem*, shadows, the word became translated more correctly as image, an image only made possible through the contrast of light and dark."

"And, as far as I remember, they didn't cover themselves with their egos, but with bikinis made from leaves. Apple leaves I assume." I chuckled at the image.

"The fruit of knowledge was not an apple. That was an interpretation created by the artists working under the auspices of the church, in an attempt to make the story more palatable to their European audiences. The real fruit of knowledge was the pomegranate, the fruit of the womb. The fruit represented the world and the seed at the center. The center of the seed itself is its essence. In order to change the entire universe, only the smallest seed needs to change. Just as a small pebble creates ripples, a small change can change the entire world. This is how you create the Garden of Eden, at the very center of the center. Make one change and create paradise on Earth."

"Didn't anyone notice this? Didn't biblical scholars try to correct this interpretation? To uncover the code?" I asked, astonished. I fell back into the sofa, throwing my hands up into the air. All these years, we were living under an illusion. When I thought of how many people fought and died for their belief of original sin, living as though humanity had something to repent for. To know that it was never that way, it was more than I could bear.

"The most hidden secrets become revealed in their time. Of course, there were those who tried to reveal the ancient secrets, and those were usually the ones who were persecuted, crucified, expelled, or went into hiding. You see, little bird, in the patriarchal society in which you have lived for the past few millennia, it was important to translate the word to rib, the fruit to an apple, and the fault to Eve. This meant that the woman was made secondary to man, made from a part of Adam that had no use or importance.

159

They suppressed Eve, suppressed the Divine Feminine. And that is what they taught the masses."

"Why would they do that? I mean, why keep people in the dark like that?"

"The Mother Goddess had written a code into the story of creation and the time to reveal that knowledge has matured. In the Garden of Eden there were two trees; The Tree of Life and the Tree of Knowledge of Good and Evil. The Tree of Life represents the sacred spheres, and of those, humanity may eat from it freely. The Tree of Life sprouts leaves that grow for the healing of nations and the Tree of Knowledge separates you from your true nature. The truth is, you are still living in the Garden of Eden. You never fell from Eden, you were never evicted from it. The truth of the matter is that you evicted divinity from Eden. Heaven exists; it is a Heaven on Earth. Those with the eyes to see will see it."

I shook my head as it all fell into place for me. "I've never understood that part of the story. Why? Why would God withhold the information from the Tree of Knowledge? I mean, why would it even be there, if they weren't allowed to eat from it. I mean, if God didn't want them to, why didn't he just move it, or evaporate it." I was leaning forward, so close to her that our knees were almost touching. I resisted the urge to touch her, to see if she was real or if I was just imagining her.

"It was Eve's code. Remember, Eve means Life. The Mother Goddess was the creator of life. Eve is the creator of that which is invisible. Eve is the longing that awakens your desires to search for fulfillment. Man cannot enter into life except through a woman;

yet, humanity cannot enter into form except through a man. The enigma contained within the Garden of Paradise, the Garden of Timeless Unity, was that men and women did not even recognize that they are different from each other. When they ate of the fruit of knowledge, they fostered the awareness of opposites. They discovered that they were different. Male and female recognized their duality. The *sin*, meaning a transference from the ideal, was a shift in their consciousness from identity with creation, to a consciousness of duality."

"So is that the next sphere? Shifting back into consciousness of our true identity?"

"The next sphere is the principle of cause and effect. Everything happens according to Universal Law. There is nothing that merely happens. There is no such thing as chance. There are various planes of cause and effect, the higher dominating the lower. By mentally rising to a higher plane, you can become a cause and not just an effect. You become the Adam and the Eve, the cause and the effect, the seed and the vessel."

"How do I do that?"

"You achieve that by embodying your ideals."

I adjusted the cushions behind me. This was all so much to take in at once. I tried to make sense of it all, but the questions just kept coming up. "What do you mean by ideals? Do you mean what I think, or what I do?"

"There are only two things you can do; conception and conviction. Conception is a creation of thought, which finds its match in the creation of form, and conviction is the effect."

"What if I think of an ideal, let's say an ideal boyfriend, and it doesn't come into form?" I mused, thinking of Shai and the attraction that I felt towards him.

"You are not thinking of an *ideal*, but rather you are thinking of an *idea*. Ideas fly around in the ether, looking for homes. Ideals are already rooted in your essence. When an idea resonates with a thought, it is because the owner of that thought attracts it with their ideals. When you search for your ideal, it answers you as if a voice has spoken to your soul."

I thought about the concept of ideas vs. ideals. Maybe I had liked the *idea* of Shai, but not the *ideal*. I had been attracted to his good looks, the way he teased me, the way he smiled at me. I had felt an intense desire towards him, but something made me resist that desire, something I couldn't quite put my finger on. I felt so relieved that I'd rejected his advances when I did. If he'd come up to my room, he probably would have succeeded in convincing me not to come here, to find Sophia.

And then there was Ben. If it hadn't been for Ben, I wouldn't be here now. I would probably be safe in my room in Tel Aviv, safely nestled away from the calamity that was occurring in the Jerusalem streets. But, then, he knew how much I wanted to find Sophia.

I had a sudden urge to find him. He was probably out there now, searching for me. At least, I hoped he was. I considered leaving Sophia's apartment and going to look for him. Then I remembered the chaos outside and decided against it.

"How do we use the notion of embracing our ideals towards things we have no control over? For instance, how would we stop the violence in the streets?"

"There is only one power in the world that can separate conception and conviction and that is the power of decision. All else follows."

"So if I just decide to stop all the violence, all the hatred, all the war, then it just will?"

"The word—decide, comes from the Latin, *decidere*, literally meaning to cut off. When you decide, you cut off all other choices and those elements no longer exist in your reality. If they no longer exist, they must be replaced by other thoughts, other decisions. New ideas must become conceived in accordance with your convictions."

"Okay, I can see that for my personal life, but how do I convince everyone around me to share the same ideas and same ideals?"

"There will always be differences in ideas," Sophia answered. "But the day will come when humanity will all share one ideal. You must create positive ideals only. Make the world within beautiful and peaceful and the world without will express and manifest that reality. The Universe is the source and fountain of all energy and substance. The individual is simply the channel for the distribution of that energy. The beauty of the universe is revealed through the beauty of the decision; the power of the universe is revealed through the power of the decision. You must first have the knowledge of your beauty, second, the wisdom of your power, thirdly, you must understand the strength of your ideals."

Sophia's words hit me hard. I closed my eyes and mulled them over. The thing that impacted me most was also the thing that scared me most. It came not from the fear that she was wrong, but from the fear that she was right. The fear that I alone could access all of the power I secretly knew I possessed. The fear that I would discover that I was more than I thought I was. The fear that if I actually had the talent that my silent, small voice tried to convince me of, I would have to acknowledge it. And in acknowledging it, it would estrange me from all that I knew. If I embraced my ideals, then I must prove that I was worthy of them. And that scared the hell out of me.

CHAPTER 15

Thursday morning, September 29ᵗʰ
Old City of Jerusalem

Finding a shaded spot on the side of the stone steps, I began to write in my notebook. My hand let loose a torrent of thoughts I didn't even realize were in my mind. My pen, as if guided by an unseen force, wrote what my voice could not articulate. My fears, my loneliness, my hopes, all captured in a way that had never been unleashed, but, once freed, they came in a flood. Like a dam, naturally eroding to the point of demise, my mind could not keep up with the outpouring of words. Unencumbered and unchained, those words marked the pages of my notebook and the gulf of my soul. The energy emitted from the steps I was sitting on was palpable. It swirled within me, creating a whirlwind of emotion in its wake.

I don't know how long I sat there, maybe hours, maybe minutes. When the trance lifted, I brought my head up. Turning to stretch my neck, I noticed someone else sitting on the steps, two stairs above me.

He was dressed much like me—jeans and a t-shirt—yet I could tell he wasn't a tourist. He was much too comfortable in this environment to be a tourist, sitting on the step with one elbow perched on the step above. He looked like he was taking in the view of his backyard.

He caught me looking at him and smiled timidly. I returned the gesture. I couldn't tell from where, but he seemed familiar, like someone I had seen before. Maybe he was a passenger on my flight, or maybe he was on the Sherut bus with me. I tried to remember but couldn't quite place it.

For the next few minutes, I tried to work up the courage to talk to him, to find out where I knew him from. I considered asking if he was part of Natalie's Conduits of Consciousness group, to ask him about the Nevea, but the words were elusive. Finally, I began to speak, at the exact moment as he began asking me something.

"Sorry, go ahead…" I laughed nervously.

"No, no, sorry, you go ahead," he mumbled.

"I was just going to ask if you…I mean, if you're part of the… well, if you know Natalie Rose?"

His eyes lit up. "You know Natalie? Are you a friend of hers?" His interest was apparent, elevated by his ambiguous accent. I couldn't distinguish it, maybe English, maybe Australian or South African. It was hard to tell.

"Not a friend exactly…I met her on the flight here. She told me about the group that she's meeting. She invited me to come."

"Ah, yeah." He answered in his charming brogue. "I'm glad to hear she's back. I don't doubt I'll see her here."

"Are you here often?" I wondered, surprised at his comfort with this city that seemed so otherworldly to me.

"Yeah, I try to come into the Old City as often as I can. It keeps the powers-that-be on their toes. At least, I hope it does."

"What do you mean?"

"A few of us peace workers try to ensure that the political situation here remains at equilibrium. So, while the politicians elude the masses, we make certain that peace is retained in the reality of the streets."

"How do you do that?" I asked, genuinely intrigued.

"Primarily, we hope our presence is a deterrent, a constant reminder that there are impartial eyes watching. So if one side or the other tries to take any drastic steps, they know that we will know about it. But, more so, we feel that our peaceful presence here balances the otherwise biased energies."

He smiled unassumingly, as if trying to downplay the power of his words. I melted at his humility. It was the single most attractive characteristic I had ever seen in a man.

"Are you part of the media? Do you report what happens here? Isn't bad press enough of a deterrent?"

He shook his head, his hand sweeping the brown hair that fell onto his forehead. "Not really, the media is reactive. What we do is proactive. We prevent the story from happening, well, at least we try. The media, those hacks only swoop in when something has already happened, to cover a story, an incursion. And even then, they always tell it with a slant. It's actually in the interest of the media to see things happen, to sell the story. The news media are instigators, the pariah of politics. After all, riots bring ratings."

"Wow, I never thought of it that way," I remarked.

"Not many people do. I didn't either, until I lived it."

"What do you mean?"

"Do you mind if I sit closer to you?" he asked, moving to my step when I nodded acquiescence. Once he was sitting beside me, I noticed his subtle features—straight nose, framed by pale, freckled skin, blue eyes flecked with hints of grey. Definitely attractive, but in an understated, endearing way.

"I used to be one of those vultures," he continued, "used to spend my days at the American Colony, just like them. We would perch, waiting with anticipation for something to happen, to be the ones to break the news. And if there was nothing to report, our editors would start to bear down, pressuring us to get a story, something news-worthy." He paused, as if considering his words. "So, once in a while the pressure would get to one of us. Someone, usually the rookies, the ones ready and eager to make their mark in the world of news journalism, would start to look for action, start to hope for violence. And during the really dry spells, we would go in and incite some locals, start some fires. I became just like them, drinking myself to numbness, doing anything not to confront that I was part of the problem."

"And then what happened? What changed?" I tilted my head to one side, my lips in a perpetual smile.

A smile crept across his whole face, raising his cheekbones to meet his eyes.

"I met Natalie." He turned to look straight at me. "Just like you did."

He held my gaze for a long time. I tried to decipher his cryptic response, to determine what his meeting with Natalie signified. I suspected it was something romantic. A pang of envy surprised me.

"And now?" I asked.

"Well, now I'm part of the group of Light workers. We call ourselves the Conduits of Consciousness. We join forces with all of the other peace organizations, or anyone committed to the pursuit of peace. We hold vigils in tense places, ensure that the energy scales never become so inclined towards violence that the teeter-totter tips. You'd be surprised how effective it is. At first, I thought it was a bunch of crock. Praying, meditating or holding a space of peace while everything is going to shit all around you. But I've come to see it for myself. That first time Natalie brought me in, we all gathered in Jerusalem, a group of us in every one of the four quarters and set our intentions for peace and…well, I can't describe it any other way than to say, we *felt* it. We felt a shift in the awareness, a shift in the consciousness of the place. It was as if the very molecules of the hostile air were replaced by loving, peaceful atoms. I'm sure we diverted a major crisis that time."

"That's inspiring. I admire you."

"In a world under constant renovations, the contribution of every individual matters. Especially in this place." He lifted his hand to gesture towards the crowd.

"What do you mean?" I asked, my eyes looking at the wall, with its men and women sections cordoned off by a brick demi-wall.

"Well, the word Jerusalem, in Hebrew, is *Yerushalayim*. It means—they will see peace."

His words made an impact on me. Hadn't I just meditated on the words *know peace*? Hadn't I considered the philosophy of peace just that morning? He smiled at me reassuringly.

"I'm Ben." He held his hand out to shake mine.

"Selena," I responded.

"So you've read Natalie's book?"

I laughed. "Almost. I passed it on before I could finish it."

"That's good. The book is powerful. It changes people's lives, has them explore the paradigms of their beliefs. It's good that you passed it on. We need as many people turned on to it as possible. What have been your signs?"

I breathed a sigh of relief. It felt good to have someone understand, felt good not to have to justify or feel like I was crazy for seeing signs. So I told him about my reticence, my disbelief, the graffiti, the moon from last night, Hanan. I told him about my journey here and the compulsion I felt, without really knowing why. Finally, I told him about the *bulbul* that seemed to follow me, even followed me here.

"Ah, the *bulbul*...the subject of the *ghazal* by Rumi..." Ben exhaled.

"Who?"

"Rumi...a Sufi mystic, he wrote a poem about the *bulbul* falling in love with the rose."

"Funny, I just heard that story yesterday." Astounded by the amount of synchronicities, of signs.

"Rumi is one of my favorite poets. He wrote:

You were born with goodness and trust.
You were born with ideals and dreams.
You were born with greatness.
You were born with wings.
You are not meant for crawling, so don't.
You have wings. Learn to use them and fly."

The air between us was electric. I resisted the urge to write the poem down in my book, to try and commit it to memory. I turned the lines, their simplicity and power, over and over in my head.

Our eyes locked. Again, the overwhelming feeling that I knew him from somewhere washed over me, but I couldn't figure out from where. He leaned closer to me, his hand reached towards me, and for a moment, I was sure he was leaning in to kiss me.

"Did you lose this?" he asked, as he picked up a glimmering crystal from the crack in the stone and handed it to me.

It was an earring, a small teardrop-shaped purple stone. I shook my head as I turned it between my fingers.

"Maybe another sign?" he mused.

"Maybe."

We smiled at each other for a moment; then, both of us looked away in embarrassment.

"So, have you been searching for a long time for the Shekinah?" he asked, breaking the awkward silence.

"The who?"

"Oh, I guess you didn't get that far into the book. The Shekinah, the feminine aspect of God. The Divine Presence, in exile from itself," Ben answered.

I was still perplexed.

"You see," sensing my confusion, he began to clarify. "After the destruction of the Temple, and the expulsion of the people, it was said that the Shekinah also went into exile, accompanying the people," he explained. "It is told that the Shekinah lived amongst the people, but they weren't aware of her presence. It is the Hieros-Gamos, the sacred marriage between El, and his twin Asherah, whose symbol is the tree. The metaphor of Eden, which is simply Hebrew for delight, is the metaphor for the paradise of the hunter-gatherers, who had freedom, to fall into the toil of agriculture. The shift from a belief in the unity of humanity with the cycles of the Earth, to the assumption of dominion over the Earth. They say that in the end of days, the apocalypse…"

"Do you mean the end of the world?" I interrupted, remembering what Shai had said about the crazy people who come to Jerusalem thinking they are the Messiah, people who fall under the spell of the Jerusalem syndrome.

"Not at all. Most people think the apocalypse means 'the end of the world,' but in actuality it means to reveal or disclose to certain people. Even the word 'messiah' means messenger. So, the 'messengers' are going to receive information about the future that's hidden from the mass of humankind. The 'end of days' really signifies a time when the world will no longer behave in the way they have been conditioned to behave. When the old, obsolete paradigms of perception fall away and a new shift occurs in human consciousness."

That explanation didn't seem as weird as Shai had described it.

"So why do so many people believe that the world will end in the apocalypse?"

"The traditional, dogmatic religions kept the illusion of the apocalypse as the end of the world because fear is a great controller. They espoused the idea of Heaven; if you follow their faith, Hell and eternal damnation to anyone who didn't."

"So you don't believe in Heaven and Hell?" I asked, shocking myself by my own candor. A feeling of déjà-vu swept over me. It was a strange, insistent knowledge of his face, in this place, having this conversation. I considered telling him, but thought better of it.

"Heaven, Hell, even the Temple are not physical places with sensory attributes. They're metaphors for the worlds within us. The legend tells that in the End of Days, the Messiah, the messenger, will come and the Temple can be restored. When that happens, the Shekinah will come out of exile and the Temple will be rebuilt. But, it's really only a metaphor for reconciling our dual natures; the feminine with the masculine, reintegrating the male and female into the Temple within." His hands danced as he spoke, finally coming together, steepled in front of him.

"I like that." I smiled.

His blue-grey eyes twinkled with amusement. He lowered his eyelids, his long eyelashes obscuring his eyes. He gave a modest shrug of his shoulders, while his head tilted to one side. The gesture was enchanting.

"Would you like me to show you around?" he asked with boyish charm.

I grinned. "I'd love that." I answered, surprising myself as I did. I was struck with the irony that I was livid when the bus driver offered to take me, and then rebuked Shai's insistence to escort me, but now with Ben, I earnestly appreciated his offer.

When we stood, I noticed he was much taller than he had seemed at first, a full head taller than me. He led the way through another security check-point, chatting amiably the whole way. I was so enraptured listening to him that I didn't even notice the condensed market corridors. He was a wealth of information about the place and its history. He explained the basic structure of the city and how the four quarters were unevenly divided between Jewish, Christian, Armenian and Moslem. He described how the city had been razed and rebuilt repeatedly, each time by a different culture, with different ideas about what the city of Jerusalem should be. He enlightened me about the confusion of the city, the mosaic of religions, the uniqueness of the land. The narrow streets that had seemed imposing and threatening earlier, now seemed colorful and sun-filled. Ben walked through Jerusalem not as a foreigner, but as a living, breathing part of the city. He joked with the vendors in the market stalls, waved and shook hands with the locals in the streets, greeted many of them with *Salaam Achi,* as they did back to him. Walking through the Old City with Ben, I felt safe.

Finally, he brought me to the Via Dolorosa, a street unlike the closed-in, narrow marketplace corridors. We passed the purple butterfly lady and the assemblage of orange shirts, who were clustered under a circular plaque in the wall with the Roman numeral VII. There were groups of religious pilgrims from all over the world, and I overheard a myriad of languages as we passed by.

"What is everyone here for?" I asked.

"They all come to visit the Church of the Holy Sepulchre."

"What's that?"

"It's where they claim the crucifixion and burial of Jesus occurred. This street, the Via Dolorosa, means the Way of Sorrows, the road Jesus was said to have carried the cross to be crucified. It's demarcated by the fourteen stations of the cross, the significant stops Jesus made along the way, the Passion of the Christ, starting at the top of the hill and coming down into the area where the Church now stands," he told me as he led the way. He offered me the crook of his arm, through which I slipped my hand as we walked and talked. He taught me the whole history, as we strolled amiably.

We came into the church and found a spot away from the maddening crowd of tourists who were all waiting to enter a grotto of sorts.

"What are they all lining up for?" I asked.

"That's apparently the place Jesus was buried."

"And you don't think it was here?"

"Well, the evidence contradicts it, for sure. Some scholars have found proof, substantiating that the real place of the burial is at the Garden Tomb, outside of the city walls, of course there's speculation that there is no burial spot at all. But, the powers-that-be declared the Church of the Holy Sepulchre to be the place and for centuries anyone who disagreed would be tried for heresy and killed."

My eyes widened. "Wow, that's just not right. Why do they think it's here?"

"Hmmm." He chuckled as we entered through the gates back into the courtyard of the Church. "Well, that's an interesting story. You see, in the early fourth century, the Roman emperor, Constantine's mother, Helena, came here to try to find the place of the crucifixion and burial. It was said that Constantine, as a new convert to Christianity, had visions and dreams about the place of Jesus's crucifixion. Of course, there's plenty of speculation as to why Constantine converted to follow Christ. Most historical scholars think it was just a ruse to consolidate his stronghold in the region."

"Why? Were most of the people here Christian?"

He shook his head. "Not exactly. In the time between the Roman expulsion of the Jews, which sent them into exile, and the time of Constantine's conversion, many differing tribes and factions sprang up. We're talking over two hundred years of expulsion. So, a lot of information was lost, misinterpreted or hidden. There were factions of Jews living in the region, and many living in enclaves along the area of the Dead Sea, who continued to record the words of someone they called the Teacher of Righteousness. Just like the writings of the Gnostics and the Essenes. Have you heard of the scrolls that were discovered in recent years?"

"A little." I smiled, thinking of the coincidence of meeting Shai the night before, and then Hanan bringing it up again today.

"At the time of Constantine's conversion, at the Council of Nicaea in 325 CE, the Roman emperor made Christianity the state religion of Rome and it became the Roman Catholic Church. They interpreted the canon and adopted the Pauline view, the epistles based on the teachings of Paul, the self-proclaimed apostle who never met or was an eyewitness to any part of Christ's life. It meant they got to choose what went into the Bible. More importantly, they got to choose what stayed out, which meant all the bits that didn't serve them, or gave the people any power to question. They made sure especially not to retain any of the parts written by women. Then, by fear and persecution, they enforced their interpretation on the people. So, the main factions that the Roman Empire had to contend with were the Judaic tribes, the members of Jesus's relatives who were headquartered in Jerusalem. The battle for control of the Christian Church has been ongoing ever since."

"So, why did Constantine's mother choose this place?"

"Well, that is where the story gets juicy." He winked at me as he spoke. "When she came to Jerusalem in 326 CE, she was already an old woman. She asked the locals to help her, but no one would. Centuries had passed since the crucifixion and the years of battles had changed the landscape drastically. Just when Helena started to assume there was no one who knew, one man named Judas…"

I held up a hand to interrupt him. "Wait, isn't Judas the name of the man who betrayed Jesus and gave his identity to the authorities?"

"Do you believe in coincidences, Selena?"

"I'm starting not to." I chuckled. "Synchronicities, more like it."

Ben smiled at me. "It's synchronicity, all right. Did you know that a parchment called the Gospel of Judas was found recently?"

I stopped to face him. "Wow, what are the chances?" I wondered aloud, alluding to the chance of meeting Shai, Hanan, and now Ben, who all talked about these secret scrolls. It was beginning to get too weird.

"I know. Pretty astonishing, huh?"

"That's putting it mildly." I giggled. "Was it the same Judas?"

"Unlikely. I mean, there were a couple of centuries between them. The one who lived in the time of Jesus was Judas, and according to the story found in the scroll of Judas, his actions were not a betrayal at all, but a well-executed plan between them. The man who led Helena to this spot was also named Judas."

"I'm floored. What a weird twist of fate." I shook my head from side to side, looking in his eyes the whole time.

"To make matters even more baffling ...helping Helena find the site of the crucifixion earned Judas the position of the bishop of Jerusalem."

"Sounds like a good incentive to show her around."

Ben nodded. "You got it. Judas told her that the placement of the burial site and the crucifixion site had been handed down to him through family secrets. He unearthed three wooden crosses, and he identified one of them as the True Cross by scratching the arm of a sick man and watching him become miraculously healed." He put two fingers in the air, as if to say quote-unquote, to show that he didn't really believe it was a miracle.

Our elbows grazed, and I felt a surge of electricity through me. I stepped closer to him.

"Did Helena believe him?"

"Obviously." He gestured towards the throngs of people making their way into the Church to pay homage to the sacred space.

"So, what was this place originally?"

"It was a temple honoring the Goddess Venus, the goddess of love."

His gentle pronunciation of the word "love" sent shivers down my spine. I giggled nervously, berating myself for being so awkward and silly.

"Why didn't anyone find this out?"

"Politics, mainly. Over the years, the area had been razed and demolished numerous times, then in the twelfth century, the Crusaders came and rebuilt the Church over the ruins of Helena's Church and over whatever burial site remained underneath it. The Crusaders were adamant in their excavations, believing that the treasure of the Temple was hidden somewhere under all of the damage and debris. There are many legends that persist even to this day that something lies under all of these years of rocks piling up. There are many people who believe that one day a new discovery will be found that will rock the very foundation of our current beliefs."

The hair on my arms and the back of my neck tingled. I thought of what Shai had said about his determination to uncover the treasure that was eluded to in the copper scroll. I tried to connect the dots.

"Do you believe there is a hidden treasure buried somewhere here?"

Ben opened his mouth to say something, but a beeping sound interrupted him. He unclipped his pager from his belt and read the scrolling message on the screen. Within the space of a few seconds, his face transformed. His normally delicate and unassuming features took on a pensive and foreboding cloud. Before I could even say anything, he was up and running.

"What's happening?" I asked as I raced behind him. He put his arm around me, shielding me from the crowd of pilgrims. He was surprisingly strong. He held me so close that I could smell him, a mix of Turkish coffee, sweetness and determination.

"There is something happening on the grounds of the *Haram al-Sharif.* A politician is entering the grounds with thousands of riot police," he muttered quickly, his eyes already searching the panorama, assessing the shortest route.

We ran back into the maze of market stall lanes. Throngs of locals started frantically yelling in Arabic, abandoning their shop-fronts and running into the streets. I kept closely beside Ben, grateful to be protected by him.

"This is bad," he said.

He took the words right out of my thoughts.

CHAPTER 16

Thursday morning, September 29th, 2000
Police Headquarters, Old City of Jerusalem

The Prime Minister, surrounded by his attaché and security detail, rushed towards the police headquarters situated on the perimeter walls of the Old City. He knew he needed to act quickly and decisively.

He penetrated into the ranks of soldiers waiting for marching orders outside and entered into the building. He found the Old Soldier in one of the offices in the back, leaning heavily on the desk, strategizing with the police chief.

"There is a change of plan." The Prime Minister announced, trying to sound as resolute as possible, as he approached the doorway. "The operation is annulled. You will cancel and rescind orders immediately."

The two men squared off for a long moment. The Old Soldier's position did not change, though his face slowly turned a crimson color that began at his neck and reached his ears. His gaze was one of maniacal contempt, a look of loathing rarely seen in diplomatic communities.

"It is too late, Mr. Prime Minister." He sputtered the words as if acid were burning his tongue. "The men are positioned.

As are the camera crews. You conceded. I will continue my mission."

The police chief looked between the two men engaged in this duel, knowing full well the history between them. He knew also, which of the two men would be the defeated one.

"There has been a change. We have received intelligence that they will use this move as an excuse for an escalation of violence. My administration will not tolerate an act of such aggressive magnitude. I have been in communication with the Secretary-General and have been assured that the situation remains reconciliatory. I will not abide by your blatant disregard for my authority while I am in office." The Prime Minister orated the speech he had carefully rehearsed.

The Old Soldier straightened. He stepped towards the Prime Minister. When he was face to face with him, with their noses practically touching, he spat, "Your time in office is coming to an end."

And with that, the Old Soldier marched past the Prime Minister, barked at the Police Chief the command to call his retinue into order, and proceeded to lead them towards the dome.

CHAPTER 17

Thursday morning, September 29ᵗʰ
Old City of Jerusalem

"Where are we going?" I asked as we sped through the city's winding streets.

"To the *madrassa*." Sensing my hesitation, Ben added, "Don't worry, it's safe."

"Why there?" I asked, as I tried to keep up with him.

"We'll be able to see what's happening from there." I thought better of asking again. Ben's demeanor had shifted into action mode. Something big was happening. I just didn't know how big yet.

He guided me through the ancient, fortressed city lanes. Tour guides, sensing the danger, were busy corralling their groups and heading out, while locals hurriedly rushed by, trying to either get into the action or out of it. We climbed up a set of stone steps, through a gate, into an open expansive courtyard conveniently elevated above the kerfuffle of the streets.

"What is this place?" I asked.

"It used to be Pontius Pilates's praetorium. Now it's a school," he responded as he ushered me to an arched window.

I looked around the open courtyard. It was made of heavy, sand-colored stone just like the rest of the city, but along one wall, the happy colors of childhood hung like flags. The doorways to the classrooms were closed, adorned with art made by little hands. On one door there was a picture of a rainbow, its multi-hued arc gleaming in front of a big, smiley-faced, yellow sun. All along the windowed walls of the classes were more pictures, some of animals, houses and children playing in green fields with flowers. Teachers proudly displayed their student's work, just like any other school. There weren't any children there. They must have gone home for the day already.

"What do you mean it used to be a planetarium?"

Ben gave me a bemused look. He was somewhat calmer now that we were here. But, I could tell he was uneasy about something. He kept looking out of the window enclosures to the grounds below. "Not planetarium. Praetorium. It was used as the palace, the place where Pontius Pilates is said to have condemned Jesus to death. It is the First Station of the Cross on the Via Dolorosa."

I sat on the ledge of one of the vaulted openings and looked out. The cavity was open to the grounds below but enforced with rusted metal gridiron. Through the iron lattice, the view of the *Haram al-Sharif* was spectacular. It made me wish Ben could have brought me under different circumstances, safer ones.

"Great view," I said, but I didn't think Ben heard me because his eyes were fixed on the grounds in front of us.

Below marching were literally hundreds, maybe even thousands of uniformed guards, machine guns strapped across their bodies, purple berets sat askew atop hundreds of heads. In the middle of the swarm, leading the charge from within, was a large man, white-haired and bullish. He walked with an air of authority, like a military general. He carried with him an aura of entitlement. Watching this play out in front of me was surreal. I felt like I was watching a scene from a movie.

A loud, retaliatory roar erupted from the crowd of people meeting the onslaught of soldiers. An angry blockade of civilians tried to stop the general and his entourage by standing in their way, creating a human barge. The local men began to yell and gesture wildly and the women raised their arms in protest, but the general ignored them, marching right past them as he continued in.

"Selena, I have to go," Ben said briskly but apologetically. "I don't feel right about leaving you here, but I have to go help."

"I'll come with you." I stood up defiantly. We were standing face to face, staring at each other.

"No, Selena, it's not safe for you."

His statement infuriated me. He was just like Shai, forbidding me from coming to Jerusalem by myself.

"And it's safe for you?" I challenged.

"It's different for me. You're, well, you're…"

"What? Because you're a man? It's somehow safer for you?"

"No, Selena. That's not it."

"What? You don't think I could handle it?"

"No Selena, it's not that."

"What is it then?"

"It's just that you're so…so…" he paused and searched for his words. Finally, he looked straight into my eyes, his eyes shielded by his lashes. Blushing, he said, "…special."

The word took me by surprise, and I didn't argue anymore.

"I'll come right back for you." He took a few backward steps. "Please, wait here for me," he added, calling over his shoulder as he ran back down the stairs and towards the riots.

I waited a few minutes, ensuring that he was out of sight and then I followed him. Back in the streets, I walked against the onslaught of tourists making their way out. The purple butterfly lady was hastily rushing the Japanese group along. I tried to remember which way Ben had taken us. My sense of direction became jumbled and confused.

Suddenly, there were the soldiers, walking towards me, using their rifles as pointers to direct the tourists out of the city. As they approached, I couldn't believe my eyes, but it was unmistakable. The tall one, under his helmet, was undeniably Shai. A feeling of gratitude coursed through me. I ran towards him, but as I approached, I sensed something was wrong.

"You can't go that way, miss..." his partner instructed.

I looked at Shai, but he would not return my gaze. He kept his eyes dispassionately looking ahead.

"You have to leave now, miss. It is not safe here," his partner repeated.

I glared at Shai, willing him to look at me.

"Shai?"

But he still wouldn't meet my gaze. I tried again, "Shai, it's me, Selena!" Still he wouldn't respond. "Why won't you look at me?"

"*Mi zot?*" his partner asked him.

"She's no one," Shai replied to his partner, in English. "Just another one of those crazy people who caught the Jerusalem Syndrome." His eyes would still not meet mine.

I stood dumbfounded.

"Shai, we met last night! Remember, at the beach? The drum circle? The eclipse?" I restrained myself from saying, *the kiss*.

No answer.

"Time to go, miss," his partner ventured again.

My feet felt like dead weights, anchored to the ground. I couldn't move. I was mortified.

"I am not crazy!" I yelled defensively.

People peered at me as they passed by, obviously intrigued by the spectacle.

"Did you hear me? You have to go now," the partner commanded.

Then, as if out of nowhere, Ben was there. I don't know how long he'd been watching, but his blue-grey eyes exposed a shade of hurt, a tinge of betrayal. He took my arm, leading me away like some frail, deranged lunatic and brought me to the gate. I followed the mass of people leaving Jerusalem.

The chaos of the Old City permeated outside of the perimeter walls. Tourists, relieved to get out of the madness, were quick to get into taxis, or buses, or to walk as far away from the Old City of Jerusalem as possible. Locals vied to get into the Old City, some to protect their children and homes, some to form a united front against the coming onslaught.

Ben led me away silently. I knew he wanted to go back in to help his Conduits of Consciousness friends stabilize the energy towards peace.

"I don't need an escort. You can go back in."

He tightened his lips, not letting go of my arm. "I'm not leaving you alone."

"Why? What do you think is going to happen to me?"

"It's not that..."

"I'm a big girl! I can handle myself! I have been for this long, and I certainly don't need you to swoop in and save me now..."

"It's not that..." he tried again.

Angry words spilled out of my mouth like a torrent. "What? Do you think I'm going to sneak back into that craziness? Do you think I'm crazy, too? Men, fucking men! I'm not like you, Ben. I don't go looking for trouble."

"It's not that." He said insistently. He stopped me with his blue-grey eyes. He looked at me so gently and intently, I felt my reserves melt away. "Selena, I know what you're looking for..."

His words took me aback. I had forgotten about the Nevea, the mystery woman I had been searching for. In all of the turbulence, I had forgotten the purpose of coming to Jerusalem. Or, did he mean Shai? Did he think I was searching for Shai? I tried to explain myself, but the embarrassment of Shai's rejection stung like bitter little bee jabs in my throat.

Ben must have sensed my confusion because he said, "Don't worry. You don't have to explain. I'll show you the way back in."

He took me to another entrance gate, smaller and less expansive than the others, hidden behind a grove of olive trees. If he hadn't brought me there, I wouldn't even have known there was a gate there at all.

"We can go in here."

"Ben." I stopped him before he entered back into the fray of the Old City. "I really appreciate your help, but I have to do this on my own."

"Selena, I don't think you understand. It's much too dangerous for you in there right now."

"Ben, please don't patronize me. I'm not the scared little girl that you've imagined me to be. I can really handle myself."

Ben started to laugh, which infuriated me even more.

"What are you laughing about?"

"You."

I glared at him. "What's that supposed to mean?"

"I'm not the one who has imagined you to be anything. It's you. You're so busy proving that you are some strong, independent woman that you don't even see when someone is legitimately trying to help you."

"So you don't intend to go in with me?"

"Oh, I definitely intend to go in with you."

"What? Why?"

"You can't just go into certain parts of the Old City by yourself looking like you do. You'll stick out like a sore thumb. If the locals don't kick you out then the soldiers surely will."

"What do you mean, looking like I do?"

"Looking so, well, Western."

I looked down at my jeans and running shoes. They looked pretty normal to me. Then an idea dawned on me. I pulled out Hanan's scarf and tossed it over my head. Ben's eyes lit up in unspoken amusement.

"That just might do." He grinned. "But you can't just hold it in place with your hand. Do you have something to secure with?"

I opened my palm and revealed the small purple earring. In all of the commotion, I hadn't realized that I had been clutching it the whole time. The indent of the little teardrop pressed into my hand. I used it to clip the fabric of the headscarf under my chin.

Ben beamed. "You could have fooled me. But I still think I should go in with you."

"Ben, I really need to do this on my own," I began explaining, thinking of the question I wanted to ask the Nevea. "My whole life I've been playing it safe. I never went out on a limb, never rocked the boat. I've never really had any adventures. I've been hiding in the shadows for much too long. I need to do this for myself. I need to prove to myself that I can do this. I want to find the Nevea on my own."

His eyes softened. He looked at me, blue-grey eyes glistening, and I knew he understood me. Then he began his instructions to me. "Make sure you keep your eyes downcast. Keep your shoulders down. Appear more diminutive. Try not to walk so proud. And Selena," he paused, "please, please try to stay out of trouble."

We stood face to face for a long time. Neither of us could think of anything else to say; neither of us wanted to part ways.

A part of me regretted preventing him from coming with me, and I even considered suggesting that he join me. But then I thought of Shai. I didn't want to embarrass myself in front of Ben again if I were to bump into Shai. I swore to myself that if I saw Shai again, I would ignore him, just like he ignored me.

I took a step away from Ben, and then impulsively, I reached out to him and put my arms around him. His strong, tender arms enveloped me. I breathed in the scent of his body, the mixed spices of coffee and cardamom, etching the memory of him into my mind. I wondered if I would ever see him again and felt a stab in my heart at the thought that I wouldn't. The thought made me squeeze him a little tighter. I could feel the pounding of his heart against my chest, or was it mine against his? Our deep inhalations and exhalations were in tempo. We were breathing in sync. I felt a gentle heat in my heart, an expansion like a growing orb of light. And I knew, in that moment, that Ben had touched my soul.

"Go in peace, Selena. Be in peace," he whispered in my ear, before we finally pulled apart.

We stood, face-to-face, hands entwined in front of us for a few more breaths. At last, I released my hands and turned away. I left the shade of the olive trees and headed towards the stone city. As I walked away, Ben called out to me one more time.

"Selena."

I turned to face him.

"I hope you find whatever it is you're looking for."

I gave him a final nod and entered the gate.

Chapter 18

Thursday, September 29th, 2000
The Chairman's Compound, Ramallah

The Chairman was seated in the formal dining room, in the private estate located within the walls of his compound. Joining him were his public relations officers, his media advisors and several executives from sympathetic news channels.

The men were so entrenched in the feast and the strategy that none of them noticed the sound of uneven footsteps on the marbled floors of the great hall.

The Secretary-General entered the dining room, his dependency on his cane accentuated by the long strides he had to make to cross the room.

Only once he finally reached the long table and had the full attention of the men in attendance did he begin to speak. "Gentlemen, Chairman," he nodded courteously towards each man in attendance, "with all due respect I have come to caution you of the diplomatic perils of this move."

The men sat in stone silence. The imperceptible sound of the grand clock ticked the rhythm of a few beats. The men turned their astonished faces towards the Chairman, who slowly swallowed the food he had been gnawing on.

"You are not welcome here." The Chairman growled, particles of food flying with his spittle. "And your opinion is of little consequence."

"Be that as it may, Chairman, but my opinion is valid nonetheless. The short-term gain does not outweigh the long-term consequences. This is a politically calamitous move, and I cannot support it."

"I told you, you swine, your opinion does not matter. Leave now or I will have you thrown out of here!" the Chairman roared.

The Secretary-General nodded again at the stunned men seated at the table. "I hope you gentlemen may see the logic in keeping this ordeal as quiet as possible. For the sake of the future we are working towards for our children. And I hope you enjoy your lunch." He turned to leave, leaning heavily on his cane as he limped out of the dining room.

CHAPTER 19

Thursday, September, 29th
Old City of Jerusalem

As I walked back into the Old City, I felt a rush of excitement and trepidation. I tried to remember Ben's instructions, keeping my eyes down and walking less proudly, hoping that meant taking small, but hurried steps. This section of the Old City was relatively empty, as if the crowd had already moved to where the action was.

I didn't know which way to go, and I didn't want to blow my cover by bringing out my map, so I just walked aimlessly. When a patrol unit of soldiers turned into my street, I quickly made a turn into another laneway.

The headscarf created an invincible buffer zone, a sensation of security. It was comforting to be hidden and anonymous. Even if I did bump into Shai, I doubted he would have recognized me.

But within moments, my feeling of safety vanished as the thwack of propellers pulsated through the air. The helicopter was much too close, closer than a helicopter should be to the ground. The sound it emitted, amplified by the acoustics of the stone streets, was deafening. I immediately covered my ears with my hands. The cloth of the headscarf felt odd, an unusual barrier. Finding a covered portico, I went in and crouched down, sheltering myself from the ear splitting sound. The patrol unit passed by, green army fatigues tucked into burgundy colored boots. I held my breath.

Please don't find me. Please don't find me. Please don't find me.

They walked on.

I made my way down an alley, looking into the crevices that snaked and converged. Most of the tourists had gone now, and only the locals were rushing about, mostly women wearing headscarves like I was, eager to get their children to safety. Down one of the darkened lanes I saw a white veil rushing by. Hanan. I resisted the urge to scream her name. I ran towards the lane, but by the time I got to the end, she was nowhere to be seen. A mother with her two children scurried past me and turned left, so I followed her until she went into her building. The cobblestone laneway was flanked on either side by high walls, interspersed with porticos to buildings.

The sound of the helicopter chops flew away but soon remained in the near distance, this time joined by a second one, hovering even closer to the ground. In the streets, men were shouting and an occasional spray of bullets would pierce the air. I don't know how long I stayed like that, crouching in the dark portico, hoping that no one would find me. What was I thinking? Why did I do this? Foolishness weighed down on me. This took the prize for the stupidest thing I had ever done.

The sudden compulsion to pray struck me. Too bad I didn't believe in God, remembering the note I stuck into the wall.

Know peace, know peace, know peace… seemed as good a prayer as any other.

Behind me was a set of old stone stairs, leading up to an iron gate. Beyond the gate was a small landing with four doors to what must have been apartments. Three of the doors were brown, and one was painted an old, mottled blue. I contemplated knocking on one of the doors, hoping to be able to hide inside for a while, but then fear trumped that decision. I was immobilized with fear. The sound of my heartbeat in my throat rivalled the noise around me. I tried to swallow, but no saliva coated my tongue.

The beating propeller of the helicopter returned, thwacking the air like a thousand simultaneous thunderbolts. The deafening sound of bullets sprayed into the air like the mad sputter of a tank, only amplified. I jumped against the wall, eyes closed, gasping for air. I imagined someone trying to shoot down the helicopter. My thoughts ran wild with the idea that the helicopter would come crashing down on me, killing me in this stone dungeon.

The shouts seemed to be getting closer. Waves of rioters passed by, followed intermittently by bands of army patrols. Occasionally, I would hear them clash. Tear gas canisters fired and the crowds dispersed, only to reunite elsewhere and start again.

Know peace, know peace, know peace…

It began to get dark outside. The notion that night was falling put me into a state of near panic. How would I find my way out? How would I possibly stay here all night? Did I even want to find this enigmatic Nevea anymore? What had I done?

Know peace, know peace, know peace…

I don't know how long I stayed petrified in that portico. The fear was overwhelming, freezing me to that very spot.

Fuck Selena, you've got to get out of here. I screamed at myself.

Fuck. Fuck. Fuck.

I was frozen by the thought of leaving my little sanctuary, and the dark, looming streets terrified me. I wished Ben were there; he would know where to go. As soon as I thought of him, a flitting shadow caught my eye. I looked up and to my astonished eyes, there on top of the gate sat the *bulbul*.

CHAPTER 20

Thursday night, September 29th
Old City of Jerusalem

The night sky was muted through the golden-stained glass. Sophia slid open one side of the window, allowing the moon's radiance to enter. A slight breeze wafted in, a pleasant reprieve in the motionless air of the apartment.

I was apprehensive. I preferred the window closed, even though the air was stiflingly still. I felt much safer being cocooned in the safety of her apartment. I adjusted myself on the cushions, while Sophia pulled out two fans from a hidden pocket of her tunic and handed me one. With an elegant and fluid twist of her wrist, she opened her fan. But when I tried to do the same, I looked clumsy and uncoordinated. Her fan had a beautiful red leaf motif on a white background. Mine was plain brown, but the air it produced came in welcome waves.

Sophia's eyes were fixed on a far off point in the room, her fan undulating in the air. I waved my own fan in quiet contemplation. The chaos outside had calmed, though some distant yells intermittently pierced the night air.

"Tell me, all that happened earlier today, what is the 'secret message' that I should learn from it?" I asked, as I twirled a loose fiber in one of the cushions.

"Hand me that flower, little bird." Sophia pointed to the pot sitting on the window ledge.

I got up and brought it to her. I stretched and peeked out of the window, ensuring that we were far enough off the ground that nobody could climb in, before I sat back down on the sofa.

"Just as with this lily that blooms above the earth, there are very real roots doing invisible work below the earth. As above, so below. The process of this lily becoming what it was destined to become started long before it blossomed."

She turned the lily upside down and tapped on the bottom of the pot. The plant slipped out; yet, the earth remained in the cylindrical form of the pot. The roots made sinewy white veins along the sides, crisscrossing randomly and haphazardly. She held the lily upside down and placed the pot beside her.

"In the same way as the lily, within you there exists a world, a world of thoughts, feelings and powers. It exists of light and life and beauty. That world within is the mind. Thoughts of courage, power, confidence and hope all produce a corresponding state in the outside world. But there is one arch-enemy to this light and that is fear. Fear is the cloud that hides the sun, the enemy which leaves perpetual gloom."

She gently placed the lily back into the pot, delicately caressing the petals and leaves.

"Just as a flower may die, but its scent remains, the ether has retained the memory of the form. The essence of the flower has manifested its particular record in the Book of Life."

"What do you mean? What is the Book of Life?" I asked.

"In Hebrew, the word for the heavens, *shamayim,* hides within it the word *mayim,* meaning water. The letter that differentiates the two is the shin, which represents fire. So this implies that the heavens contain the fire waters from above. In Sanskrit, those superior waters are called *Akasha,* which is a force or an energy, the blue substance in the space that contains fire. So the primary forces of air, fire and water are active. The *Akashic* waters are also called Mother, within which the heavens are contained. The space within these *Akashic* waters must be filled with a material medium and that material is astral light. The future exists within the embryo of astral light, waiting to be born. Also, the present exists in the embryo of the past. But, future and past do not exist in reality, only in our narrow view of reality. There is no beginning and no end. Time is eternal as space is boundless. The past no more exists than the future. Only our memories survive. And our memories are but glimpses that we catch of reflections of astral light."

I rubbed the inside corners of my eyes, denying them their desire to close. "So, there is a place where all of the past and future scenarios exist?"

"It is not a place but a dimension. A dimension of consciousness that contains a vibrational record, a vibrational body of consciousness. All time exists simultaneously. It exists everywhere, available at all times, in all places. It is an unseen world, one that humans can only identify through experience."

"So every step we make is pre-destined? What about free will?" I asked, intrigued, albeit somewhat skeptical.

"The genesis of free will is the crystallization of your spirit. *Akasha* is the primary substance; it is the indelible quality energy before it has taken form. The *Akashic* Records are the Light Body of universal consciousness. They contain the radiant vibrations of light that are all things; human, animal, mineral and ethereal. The Records are like a blueprint for your life's journey. Every time you grow into the awareness of your soul, the Light of your Records becomes revealed to you, and you become more enlightened."

"How do we access these Records?" I asked, thinking of my mom. A pang of grief threatened to overwhelm me again.

"You will gain awareness with each delve into the Records. For now, you can access them through your dreams, your consciousness and your memories."

"What if our memories don't survive? What if we forget?" I asked, thinking of my forgotten childhood.

"Memories are not contained in your mind; therefore, they cannot be lost. The act of memory is to peek inside the tablets of astral light that are stamped into the impression of every thought you think, every act you perform and every future event."

"So we can 'remember' the future? As in telepathy? Is that how an Oracle can predict the future?"

"There is a constant interchange of energy between the visible and the invisible universes. When you remember something, you are merely visiting its astral form, glimpsing the *Akashic* records. For the Oracle, there is already a very clear picture for the eye to follow, whether in flashes of soul memory or anterior experiences."

"Is that why sometimes something, or someone, can feel so familiar? Like déjà-vu?" I asked, thinking of my connection with

Ben, and my chest expanded like it had when I'd hugged him. I hoped he was safe.

"A déjà-vu is something that has happened that seems familiar and a vu-déjà is something that seems familiar and has yet to occur."

"How can something that is yet to occur feel familiar?"

"It is familiar because you have seen the soul of the world. You have been the raindrop that falls in the river, that flows to the sea, that is pulled by the sun into a cloud, carrying with it all the wisdom of the rain, the river and the sea. Just like the raindrop, you have been reborn again and again."

"As in reincarnation, past lives?" My head was heavy and I felt a strange tingling in the base of my spine. Sleep threatened to take me, but I kept shrugging it off.

"Yes, except in your current understanding of time, reincarnation is an overly simplified explanation. Because all time—past, present and future—exists simultaneously, or in parallel. Glimpsing what you call a 'past life' is really just a glimpse into a parallel existence."

"Are you saying I've been here before? Or rather, am now here, or that is, living a parallel life on some other dimension?" I tried to iron out the implications in my mind, but it was too confusing. I didn't quite understand it. I wrestled with the whole concept, but as soon as I went down the rabbit hole, so many more questions would come up.

"For many, many lives, yes. Growing into the awareness of one's spiritual nature takes many lifetimes." She smiled at me. "You will find that if you ask of it, your memory will give you the answers. Memory holds all the keys. The mind is like the closet for a woman's dresses. Full and vibrant. The keeper of things that no longer fit but are still treasured. You have been here before, and you will be again. And in each life you have been a Story Woman."

As she said it, I felt a twinge of recognition as a distant memory suddenly opened itself up to me. I shivered from head to toe.

"Is that why you're teaching me these things? The sacred spheres?"

"Yes, little bird. I have taught you in every epoch, in every language, and I will continue to teach you."

"Will there ever be a time when I stop forgetting?"

"I will continue to return, to teach you these lessons in every lifetime. You must acknowledge your pathway and fulfill the destiny of your soul."

"What if there are things I would rather forget?"

"Those are the things you fear most; yet, those are the very same things that need to be acknowledged. Release your fears, your blame, your shame, bring them into the light, then place them lovingly onto the wings of a dove and let it fly. The bird cannot fly under the weight of your shame."

"How? How do I release those feelings that I've buried deep inside for so long?"

"Let those feelings come to the surface. Resist your tendency to submerge them into the abyss of your soul. Murky waters reveal no light."

"Then just forget them? Pretend they never happened?" I asked.

"Allow yourself to stand beside them, not within them. Become the observer of your journey, not the victim."

"So, it's not about forgive and forget?" I had to remind myself to take a deep breath. The air came in stages, the kind of breath that comes during a sob session. I tried again. Still the air eluded me. I resisted the tears. I would not give into them.

"The act of forgetting is a fallacy. Just as we don't forget our childhood, so too, does our evolution retain a spiritual memory. Future states and past states are not created; they have already happened. They are already written in the spiritual records, of which you are unaware. So you have two options; you can choose to evolve based on nature's pressures, or you can evolve naturally by developing your awareness."

"I don't remember my childhood," I said, with a familiar pang. The air was suffocating me. My early years had always drawn a blank for me. My mother constantly joked that I emerged from the womb fully grown, without ever really being a child. Maybe that was why I didn't remember anything. Or maybe it was that I preferred to forget.

"Don't expect flowers to grow in a place where no seeds have died first. Childhood memories will only last if they are woven with the finest thread, in secret places of the mind."

I visualized myself sewing my childhood memories with a very fine needle and a glimmery length of gossamer thread. Suddenly, images flooded my mind, remembrances of the beach, the moonlight, a gentle caress, a soft lullaby. The fabric of pain and anguish I let wither. I double stitched the memories of joy and laughter, and I smiled to myself, pleased with my handiwork.

"Just trust your intuition, little bird."

I heard the echoes of Natalie's voice. *"Just trust your intuition,"* she had said.

"I don't think I have intuition."

"Everyone has the dormant ability of intuition."

"Do you mean like ESP?"

"Extra sensory perception, or other such phenomena, is an explanation your world of science has given to the knowledge of things beyond your five senses. It comes from the onerous belief that what is in your human awareness is all there is. Intuition means simply opening your awareness to incorporate the world that exists outside of your sensory experience."

"How do I awaken intuition? Isn't intuition something that some people have and others don't?"

"Just the opposite. By this point in your evolution, humanity should have become aware of their capability to have developed the sense of *gnosis*, of knowing without knowledge. The developments of your evolution should have already given you the keys to the Book of Life."

"So, what's stopped us from that development?"

"Your pursuit of the Tree of Knowledge and your ignorance of the Tree of Life. It is said that the fruits of the Tree of Life are twelve, the five physical senses and the seven psychic senses of the soul. A baby in the womb still enjoys all twelve senses of the Tree of Life and has knowledge of the *Akashic* records. In the moment before the baby is born into this world of corporeality, an angel places her finger on the baby's lips and whispers 'shhh....,' and a sacred agreement is made. That is why every human has the mark of the angel on their lip."

My finger reached up to feel the little indent in my upper lip. It was a gesture I often made when I needed to think.

"If we made a sacred agreement with the angel, doesn't that mean we're not supposed to remember?"

Sophia raised both her hands in front of her and interlaced her fingers. She brought her hands to either side of her head, left and right, right and left. "Your world has placed much emphasis on rational knowledge. You have embraced the constraints of the logical mind and rescinded the wilderness of the intuitive mind. Reclaiming the knowledge of the seven forgotten fruits of the Tree of Life was the journey humanity was destined to take. Yet, you have veered wildly off course."

"So you're saying that humanity was meant to be psychic?"

She disentwined her fingers and laid them on her lap, palms up. "I am saying that humanity will unveil the light of the Book of Life when more people follow the path that their intuition lays out for them."

"Okay, so how do I awaken my intuition?" I asked.

"It is late, my little bird, and you must sleep."

I was taken aback. I hadn't even thought of staying here for the night. I thought I would leave as soon as the riots in the streets died down, that I would make my way back to Tel Aviv under the cover of darkness.

I bit my lip, a little too hard. I tried to keep the panic from bubbling up and overwhelming me. As long as Sophia kept talking, I felt safe. "You haven't finished telling me how to awaken my intuition yet!"

"Ah, but I have. It is an irony of consciousness. The moment your conscious mind sleeps, your subconscious mind, and therefore your intuition, can awaken."

"So that's it? Just going to sleep will awaken my intuition?" I desperately tried to hide the intimation of doubt from creeping into my voice, but to no avail.

"Yes. It is that simple. Your dreams will reveal to you all of the spheres, all of the heavens and all of the light. Allow your dreams to reveal to you the Book of Light."

"And then will I awaken my intuition when I am awake as well?"

"Not exactly, little bird. The Book of Life must remain closed while you explore the physical world. In order to develop your intuition during your waking hours, you must work to achieve the same level of subconscious awareness while awake as you do while you sleep. You must not only give your dreams the wings to fly, you must also give them feet to walk."

I was struck by what a different person I was today than I was yesterday. When I'd met Natalie with all her talk of magic and mystery, I relegated it to the voodoo and hoodoo of eccentric hippies. Yet, here I was, enraptured by the wisdom of this amazing woman. Now the stories didn't seem to be hippie, or woo-woo at all. A little unorthodox maybe, but not weird.

"How do I do that?" I asked.

"Lure your dreams out of their cages. Sprinkle grains and crumbs outside the door of the cage and let your dreams find comfort in their freedom. Dreams, like tamed animals, forget their wild nature. Dreams forget the feeling of the air under their wings, the rush of wind and the spray of water. The cage that has imprisoned them has become their comfort, their home. They have lost the courage, the instinct, the determination. Allow them to come to the threshold, to step out, and to become untamed. And when they have unbridled themselves from the cage, untethered themselves from logic, run wild and free, only then invite them back to you with all of the compassion and grace that a mother gives her child."

"Sophia…"

"Yes, little bird?"

"Before I go, there was one thing I wanted to ask…"

"Anything."

"Well, I was wondering if, I mean, if it's possible for you to…"

"It is all right, little bird, you can ask any question you wish. Questions are the instrument of your essence."

"I was wondering if you could talk to my mom?"

Sophia took a deep, pensive breath. She straightened her tunic over her knees. I held my breath as I choked back the tears. When she spoke, she spoke very softly. "Little bird, speaking to the dead assumes they are dead, but consciousness does not reside in the body; consciousness does not reside in your thoughts. When you die, your vessel fades, but its energetic essence continues. That spark is contained in the memories of all of those we have loved. Your mother exists in all of the memories, all of your fears, and the richness of your joy. She exists in the deepest recesses of your being. She exists in your stories. She exists in the dimensions beyond this limited one, but exist she does. She exists in your consciousness. Always has. Always will."

"So she is a part of me? I mean, of my consciousness?" I ventured.

"That's right, little bird. When you shift out of the ordinary human consciousness, you enter into the Divine universal consciousness."

"So, where does my mother..."

"All around you. You do not need anyone else to communicate with her. You just need to become aware of her, or rather, her essence. She is all around you. She speaks to you in the thoughts you think, the decisions you make, in the glint of the moon. She is every memory, every breath. Do not seek her outside of yourself. Do not seek her in the world, but seek her within for it is there that she resides."

Tears welled up in the corners of my eyes. I was suddenly struck with an exhaustion like I had never encountered. The day had been overwhelming and Sophia's soft voice was trance-like, hypnotizing me. I was curious to hear what she had to say, but I was determined not to fall asleep here.

"Sophia..."

"Yes, little bird?"

"Why did she have to die?" The question tumbled out, like an errant child, accompanied by an audible sob.

Sophia smiled at me with the corners of her lips and eyes. "All souls agree, before they come into this dimension, to their particular assignment in this realm. For your mother, the assignment she had agreed to honor came to pass, and she fulfilled her life's mission. It was her particular soul signature, the stamp she agreed to leave on this world. She brought you into existence, and led you here. That was the gift of her life. You fulfilled for her the essence of her life."

I had never thought of it this way, but I could see how true Sophia's words were. My mother had never really wanted anything else in her life. She sacrificed her career, her education, and her relationships for me. I'd always assumed that she wanted to ensure that I didn't make the same mistakes she had, and that was why she pushed me to go to school, study, get a career, be independent. Now I realized that she didn't want those things for her, she wanted them for me. School, career, academic accolades, those things wouldn't have made my mother happy. They wouldn't make me happy either. The tears were streaming down my face freely now. I didn't even make any attempt to wipe them away. They felt good, cleansing. I relaxed into the cushions of the chaise longue and took a deep breath.

"Are you ready to explore?" she asked.

"Yes." I exhaled.

"Then ask me the question you came to ask."

I thought of the question that had led me here. I thought of the last of M's letters, the one that was in an envelope, post-stamped two weeks before my birth. The words of the letter I knew by heart.

Ma Chérie Deborah,

I have grave news to tell you, though what has happened to me pales in comparison to the heartbreak I feel at not receiving any word from you. Please, write to me and tell me you are safe. My mind is turning with the possibility that I have somehow offended you, or that you don't love me anymore. I cannot know what is in your heart. If it is the case that I have wronged you, please know that it was never my intention.

The news I have for you is this: The day after I last wrote you, I went to visit the camps along the border. While I was there, a skirmish erupted and the factions began to fire into the civilian buildings. I ran for cover, finding an apartment owned by a compassionate old woman, who welcomed me in, despite not knowing who I was. Her kindness I shall never forget. She reminded me of the legends of the mysterious wise woman that my grandmother would always whisper of. That old woman taught me things in that short meeting, things that would have taken me a lifetime to awaken to. By nightfall, however, the helicopters appeared, dropping bombs on the buildings. Our building was hit. I do not know what happened after that. I awoke weeks later in the hospital, my leg amputated. The kind old lady, I was later informed, did not survive.

Ma Chérie Deborah, when will this end? Why do we keep returning to the same annihilation and destruction? Why do we keep doing this? What purpose does it serve?

I am so relieved to know you are out of harm. As for me, I will keep fighting against injustice and abuse of power in whatever way I can. Though now that I am crippled, I will have to find another tactic in which to pursue peace.

I cannot know whether you are receiving my letters or not, and I hope you forgive me when I tell you I will not write to you anymore. Your silence is more than I can handle. Every day that passes without a response from you is a death for me. I will never stop hoping and awaiting a letter from you, until one day, when I may see you again.

Although it is my leg that is severed, it is my heart that I must mend.

Until then, know that you are in my thoughts, in my prayers, and in my soul,

M

P.S. Mon âme te cherchera à tout jamais.

I closed my eyes and choked back my sobs. "Please, tell me who my father is," I asked quietly.

"I will ask the Angels of the Light, of the Truth, to open the Book of Life for you." With that, Sophia began a slow incantation, a chant-like mantra. *"Mal-khei Ha'Or, Kivun Ha-Emmet, Patchu-na et Sepher ha-Chayim, Selena Silver. Ha-Sepher Patu-ach, Amen."* She repeated, *"Mal-khei Ha'Or, Kivun Ha-Emmet, Patchu-na et Sepher ha-Chayim, Selena Silver. Ha-Sepher Patu-ach, Amen. Mal-khei Ha'Or, Kivun Ha-Emmet, Patchu-na et Sepher ha-Chayim, Selena Silver. Ha-Sepher Patu-ach, Amen."*

Despite my rational determination not to, I fell asleep.

PART III

THE GIFT OF KNOWLEDGE

I am Protennoia the Thought that dwells in the light...
She who exists before the All...
I move in every creature...
I am the invisible One within the All...
I am perception and Knowledge,
Uttering a Voice by means of Thought.
I am the real Voice.

—Trimorphic Protennia
(Triple-Formed Primal Thought)
-from the texts found at Nag Hammadi

CHAPTER 21

I was flying above the streets of Jerusalem. From below came the raucous sounds of people rioting. Angry shouts, the chaos of the crowd of people, arms raised in vindictive anger. Yet, the ferocious energy of the atmosphere did not disturb me. I remained untouchable, high above them, soaring. The wind pressed against me, made way for me, became dispersed by me. I pushed against it, willed it to bend to my form. It stubbornly acquiesced, allowing me to spiral into the ether and dive into the firmament. I heard laughter, squeals of delight, the raw energy of joy; yet, there was nothing but air around me. Then I realized that the laughter had come from within me. The pure sensation of ecstasy.

Instincts took over, descending me lower, above the heads of the maddening crowd and into the gates of the Temple. The first of the gates towered high above the ground and its entire face was plated with gold. The sides were flanked by two enormous pillars, bronzed and decorated with a motif of pomegranates and topped with lilies. The men amassed in the courtyard outside demanding entrance, but their progress was stalled by armor-clad sentries. I soared towards the immense golden doors. The frame of the doors was gilded with glittering vines and grape clusters, as large as a man. I easily passed through.

Inside the hall there were clusters of men wearing long white robes and turbans, and they gathered around the seven-branched candelabrum, urgently placing loaves of bread on the table and mumbling words of prayer. The incense burning on the altar created wispy, willowy strands of smoke into the air. I continued further inside. In front of the third set of doors hung an ornate, beautiful veil made of a glorious tapestry. The textile was embroidered in blue, purple, red and plain linen. The picture created by the embroidery was a view of the heavens and earth, with the scarlet thread sewn into the fire of the upper heavens—the plain linen, the earth; the blue, the air, and the purple, the sea. I passed behind it and entered the inner sanctum where, flanked on either side by the huge outstretched wings of olive wood statues of cherubim, there was a massive rock.

To my astonished delight, behind the rock amidst a cluster of women, all draped in gauzy lilac sheaths, stood Natalie and Hanan. Natalie looked even more beautiful then ever, and Hanan was radiant, with long, black curls cascading down her back. In front of the rock, sitting regally on a beautiful, opulent throne, sat Sophia.

The women welcomed me in an enfolding embrace, and I felt the peculiar sensation of my winged body somehow morphing, transforming, shape-shifting into a human one.

We became like the flames flickering all around us. We were wisps of fire dancing and playing, igniting one another in movement. Childishly, impishly, we frolicked in tandem with each other, arms outstretched, legs languid, laughing, turning, grasping for each other. The sound of our giggles echoed off the stone walls, creating an angelic symphony. The flickering flame that was each of us became enmeshed with each other's as we came closer, untethered as we pulled away. And as we embraced and caressed each other, each singular flame became part of the greater fire. Alone we burned as an exquisite spark; together, we enflamed into a glorious blaze. Tangled in each other, we danced, our voices humming, chanting, singing and tapping, heightening and expanding, until we collapsed into each other, reveling in the vortex of our joy.

Where am I? I asked, though I knew my voice had not made a sound.

You are in the Holy of Holies, responded the voice I knew was Natalie's, and yet not Natalie's. It was the voice of what Natalie would be if Natalie took no form. It was the voice of Natalie's essence.

What is happening?

The Temple is soon to be destroyed, answered the essence of Hanan.

In that very moment, one by one, robed men trickled into the inner sanctum. They assembled before Sophia and bowed in reverence. My thoughts slowly processed what I was seeing. I confusedly tried to distinguish how it could be possible, but I recognized the first two men. They looked just like the Prime Minister and the Chairman, whose pictures appeared in the newspaper; however, that seemed to be in a different world, a different dimension. The next man assembled, and him too, I recognized. He was the old, hawkish, military general I had seen leading the political coup on the grounds of the *Haram al-Sharif.*

Mystified, I looked at the remaining men. Yes, my eyes weren't deceiving me, even with the robes, the beard and the turban, I could tell it was the driver of the crew bus, the one who told me the story of the *bulbul*. Beside him, tall and charming, was Ben. His blue-grey eyes penetrated into mine. The sense of gratitude overwhelmed me.

Thank you, I said, without saying.

His head tilted forward in a subtle, almost imperceptible nod.

My heartbeat quickened.

Next to him stood an antiquated version of Shai, his gaze fixed on me. *I'm sorry*, his eyes seemed to say. *It's alright*, I thought towards him, feeling a freedom I had never experienced before.

Who are these men? I asked Natalie.

They are the Shomrei ha-Or, the Keepers of the Light, charged in every generation to uphold the secret of the Temple, to keep the knowledge of the truth alive, the essence of Natalie responded.

Why do they all look familiar?

They each have a mission that they have been assigned in every lifetime. They are assigned to protect the secrets of the Temple.

Then why are they on opposite sides of the conflict?

Every one of them, in every lifetime, must make the realizations of their own mission for themselves. They are on what seems like opposing sides because they do not yet realize that they are on the same side.

Why did one help me find Sophia and one try to stop me from finding her?

The one who helped you has become enlightened to his essence. The one who tried to dissuade you had not yet. Yet both of them followed what they knew they must do. Each in his own way guided you to meet Sophia. They do so in every lifetime.

Of the men gathered, I recognized all but one in one way or another. Even the one I didn't recognize seemed like someone I knew somehow, or rather someone I should know.

Who is that one? I asked the essence of Natalie, directing my intention at the pleasant, smiling man with the dark eyes, the one who limped as he walked and leaned heavily on a cane.

That, Selena, is your father.

The world seemed to stop in that moment. I looked at the man. He looked much older than the picture I had found, but, yes, the same kind eyes, the same soft smile. I tried to keep calm. My reserve fell away. I willed him to look at me, and he did. His face transformed into a huge, welcoming smile, and I sensed a mutual recognition. His eyes danced, illuminated by the torchlight. My father.

My father? I asked Natalie. *Does he know?*

His soul knows. That was the agreement he made with the soul of your mother. In every lifetime, he has agreed to protect you. In this life, it was by being absent. It was the path chosen for your soul's growth, and his, and your mother's.

He turned to me and in a language that can only be described as pure love he said to me—*Ma Chérie Selena, mon âme te cherchera à tout jamais. My soul will search for you, for always.*

I sensed myself melting, dissolving into a singular drop, morphing and transmuting. Every one of my cells seemed to liquefy and become a part of everything around me.

Within moments, I felt years of defensive walls crumble. My whole life had been spent blaming him, blaming my mother, feeling sorry for myself. My whole existence revolved around how hard-done-by I was. And yet, now I realized, it was all part of the plan, part of some long forgotten pact made by the essence of my soul, in cahoots with the essence of his soul. It was all so ridiculous. Of course it had to be exactly as it was. It was divinely orchestrated. Suddenly, the word "divine" didn't bother me so much. I felt a wave of emotion spill over me, a bliss so magnificent that it engulfed me in ecstasy. I felt what can only be described as love. Pure, exquisite, unconditional love. I began to laugh, and my laughter summoned more laughter. Shrieks and hoots of joy accompanied me, erupted in me, enveloped me.

The lens over my eyes seemed to have lifted, and everything was suddenly awash in a brilliant, luminous aura. The men appeared to be full of wisdom and forgiveness, like ancient sages awaiting eager students. Sophia was glowing from within, a pulsating luminosity stretching beyond her and melding with everyone and everything else. I looked at Natalie and Hanan. They were bathed in a glorious, illuminating white light. As I glanced down at myself, I saw that I was also emitting this inner radiance. I seemed to exist in everything, and everything existed in me. *Who are we?*

This time it was the essence of Hanan that answered. *We are the Goddesses of the Moon, the North Star and of Destiny.*

The first of the men began to speak. The language was guttural, foreign to me; yet, somehow, I could understand what he was saying. He told Sophia about the riots outside, the insurgence, the imminent danger. He pleaded with her to remove the Ark, to bring it to safety. He begged her to flee while she could, to escape to safety.

Tranquil and majestic, Sophia responded:

The secrets of the Temple cannot be destroyed.

They have lived since the beginning of time and they will continue to exist beyond the end of time.

Humanity searches for the ultimate truth, and in their search, they obscure it.

People slaughter in the name of Understanding, they kill for Knowledge, they murder in lieu of Wisdom.

Yet, Understanding, Knowledge and Wisdom do not dwell in the Temple. They have always resided in Nature. Humanity has stopped looking to Nature for the ultimate truth. They will continue to do so until the day that the truth will be revealed to them.

The people will keep searching for the Temple; yet, the Temple is, and always has been, within.

Time will conceal what is now shining in splendor.

Humanity is at the precipice of a dark night.

In the new dawn, Humanity will reawaken and know a Glory unseen in the present hours.

It is then that Understanding, Knowledge and Wisdom will return to them.

It is then that I will return to them.

Go now and spread the message. Tell the story of the Temple and of the Shekinah, of Sophia, who will return only once the people seek her.

Go. Ensure the secrets are spread wherever Humanity exists for in the End of Days, the Knowledge of the Goddess will guide you.

Sophia signaled for the men to leave and waited as the last of them exited to the other side of the veil, and beyond the doorway of the inner sanctum. Once they did, Sophia retrieved a small tablet the color of Sapphire from inside her robes. With only the strength of her will, she proclaimed that the rock would rise into the air. The massive boulder began to lift slightly; then it hovered until it raised itself above our heads.

Without hesitation, Sophia walked into the cavernous opening of the space under the boulder and gently placed the Sapphire tablet in the center of the floor. The moment she walked out from under it, the rock fell heavily to the ground. The impact felt like an explosion. It caused the two cherubim to fall over onto each other, which caused the doorway to crumble, the tapestry to tear and the columns to topple. The ground beneath us began to rumble. From the depths of the Earth, a shift was occurring.

Sophia, Natalie, Hanan and I joined the other women as we calmly walked out of the inner sanctum, past the candelabrum, and anonymously melted into the cacophony of the streets.

I turned around, just in time to see the complete and utter destruction of the Temple.

CHAPTER 22

Friday morning, September 30th
Old City of Jerusalem

I awoke to the swift, shrill squaw of a bird. It took me a few minutes to catch my breath as I tried to figure out exactly where I was. On the window sill was a black raven, its opal eyes boring into me. I sat motionless, willing it to fly away.

"Ah, you have woken!" Sophia entered, balancing a tray of food. She made quick little noises with her tongue, as if beckoning a family pet.

"I see you have met my morning friend." She placed the tray on the low table and walked to the window to gingerly pet the bird. He responded by lowering his head to her hand.

"The raven. A creature with no fear in his heart, only curiosity." Sophia looked at the bird lovingly. She took a corner of bread, ripped it into pieces and placed it on the ledge. He immediately pecked at it with his beak.

"Did you sleep well?" she asked, turning to me as she did.

"Um, yes. I guess I did…I had this crazy dream. I dreamt that…" I tried to explain it, more to myself than to Sophia, but I knew that words would only limit what I felt.

The raven squawked again, even more vociferously this time.

"Shhh..." Sophia said. "The records are closed. You are in this world now. Eat a little something before you go, little bird. You must recuperate your strength because you will be leaving soon."

I was more than a little jolted by her words. After all the fear I'd felt the day before, and the safety of her shelter, I didn't really want to go back to the calamitous streets. I didn't want to leave.

"Sophia, I need to know about my dream last night. I feel like I can't even distinguish between what is real and what's imagined."

"All is real," Sophia replied. "You already exist within all levels of reality."

I thought about the journey I'd made in the night, the knowledge I had when I shifted out of my awareness. I thought about everything that I discovered in my dream. I knew it wasn't my imagination; it wasn't made up.

I pictured the man with the smiling eyes. My father. Empathy and forgiveness washed over me. Whatever I had lacked growing up was irrelevant to the love I felt for him now. Whatever had prompted my mother to keep secret from me didn't really matter anymore. She'd made her choices from the place she was at the time, and maybe one day, I would find out, or maybe I wouldn't. Either way was fine with me. I realized that my whole life had unfolded exactly as it should have.

I laughed, thinking how unlike my old self I was being. Yesterday I was so logical and reasonable. I would have never believed in this stuff. Today, I saw that there was so much more to the universe than I was aware of.

The raven made a sound unusual for a raven just then, a jabber noise that sounded remarkably like the word *time*.

"The time to go is almost upon you," Sophia said, as if translating for my benefit.

I started to get up from the chaise longue.

She gestured for me to sit back down. "No, not yet. You will be given the sign when it is safe."

"What sign?" I asked, as I gathered my belongings closer to me.

I had fallen asleep in my clothes and at some point in the night, I had somehow removed my shoes. I raised my hands to my head and realized that I had been wearing Hanan's headscarf the whole time. I reached under my chin and unclasped the earring that was holding the scarf in place. Twirling the little purple earring in between my fingers, I suddenly thought of Ben. I had the impulsive urge to run out and find him. I felt an overwhelming need to see him, to explain to him everything that had happened with Sophia, my dream, and the Temple. I wanted to look into his blue-grey eyes again and tell him, yes, I had found what I was looking for.

"Eat, little bird," Sophia repeated.

The platter was filled with thick, white yogurt, honeyed dates, thinly sliced red radishes, and crusty, braided bread. Steam mushroomed up from the teapot as Sophia poured us each a cup.

"What sign am I waiting for?" I asked again.

"Do you know the legend of the Raven?" she asked, seemingly ignoring my question.

"No." I knew that if I waited long enough, the answers to all of my questions would be encrypted into her stories, so I broke off some bread and dipped it into the yogurt as I listened.

"During the great flood," she started, "one pair of every animal was spared the certain demise of the world. The rains came down hard, shadowing the land behind heavy clouds of grey. All of the other animals were fearful to explore, all but the Raven. The Raven flew into the horizon, searching for some distant shores. When he found none, he continued to fly. The Raven circled the globe, searching for safety, looking to bring protection to humanity. Sensing that the Raven would not return, the Dove then volunteered to search for land. The journey was very difficult for the Dove, the rain beat down voraciously, and the wind whipped against her wings. Finally, through the mist, the Dove could see a faint black dot. It was the Raven, guiding her to safety. Together they found a tiny stretch of land, with a single withered tree. The Dove took a twig from the tree and brought it back for humankind. The Raven remained with the tree so that the Dove would know where to return. Ever since, the Raven has searched for his Dove. The branch is his peace offering to her."

"Is that why the dove is used as an emblem of peace?" I asked.

"The Dove is the symbol of divinely inspired peace and love from the Goddess Venus. The Raven represents the forces of giving, while the Dove represents the forces of receiving. The balance in a perfect symbiosis. Together, they translate the primal forces into words and symbols."

"And the tree?" I asked.

"You are brilliant, my little bird. Yes, the tree in this story is the Tree of Life."

"So, the dove returning with a twig from the Tree of Life means…"

"It means that the Raven, our divine masculine, awaits our return. When we return to the Tree of Life, we will reunite with the essence of our natures. We will find a new way to communicate, live at higher levels of understanding, abandon the fighting and futility of our nihilistic humanity."

Sophia carefully straightened her tunic over her knees. I picked up the last of the syrupy dates from the platter before me. Swabbing the bottom of the bowl of yogurt, I let the combination of the honeyed dates and flavor of the yogurt play on my palette.

I thought of my dream, the unbelievable feeling of flying, the rock levitating in the nothingness. My mind searched for something in its periphery, a memory of something that I didn't remember seeing, but I knew it was there. A shadow of something on top of the gate.

I tried to ask Sophia, but after the dream, my words seemed clumsy and primitive.

"Are you ready for the final lesson?"

"Yes, I am. And the seventh sphere is…?" I pretended to rap a drum roll on my knees with my fingers.

Sophia laughed with her usual grace. "The seventh and final sphere is the balance of gender. Every male has a female counterpart and every female, a male principle. The balance of the act of giving and receiving, active and passive, doing and being, in this way you repair the world. By arousal below, there is arousal above, male and female unite, desire prevails, worlds are blessed and above and below are in joy. Like this you experience the extraordinary."

"Like getting caught in the riots yesterday?" I mused.

"What you encountered yesterday was unfortunate, yes, but not extraordinary. The powers of the feminine have been in a state of disequilibrium for far too long. The lever has leaned too far to the masculine principle, making humanity seek aggression and warfare. When the balance returns to the Divine Feminine, then you will see the birth of an extraordinary humanity. The extraordinary occurs when you are true to your soul's essence and you have expanded your energy to the realm of potential. You were never meant to be ordinary. You were meant to have extraordinary experiences, unexplainable things happen in your life. Most people have been brainwashed into thinking that ordinary lives are somehow preferable. But that is not the way it is supposed to be. A life that is ordinary is not true to its soul's essence, and the soul will never experience growth. When you are true to your soul's essence, the ordinary expressions of your world begin to fall away. You start to experience things that are out of the ordinary. Things that have never existed in form before suddenly exist. People who are in your life, your career, your hobbies; all become extraordinary experiences, placed into your life in a cosmologically ordered way."

"So, more like the people I met who ushered me here?" I asked, though I already knew the answer. I thought of all of the players who came to usher me along the way, like a cosmic theater, with each playing their role.

"Yes, little bird. Your consciousness compelled you to explore your desire; it awoke within you a dormant element of your essence. Much like a lamp that dispels the darkness, your consciousness illuminated, or revealed, the way to you."

"Are you saying that I created the path that got me here?"

"You explored the inner nature of your essence, no matter how troubled the contemplation was. If you stay with it, the experience of luminosity and knowing will increase. When that happens, the nature of your consciousness will create extraordinary experiences."

"Am I supposed to live my life looking for extraordinary things to keep happening?"

"Experiencing the extraordinary means learning the lessons that come with each opportunity and growth experience. Every interaction with the world around you is an extraordinary gift, a chance to expand. You need not search for it."

"What if everybody did that? Then the extraordinary wouldn't exactly be extraordinary anymore." I looked into Sophia's eyes, and both of us knew that I already knew the answer. I just didn't want to leave yet.

"Just the opposite. If everybody transformed their inner world, it would lift humanity to previously unexplored and unexplainable reaches. Each individual's own personal transformation and the planetary transformation would be congruous. Human evolution would expand exponentially, multiplying the level of consciousness to quantum heights. All it takes is for enough of humanity to create an acceleration effect."

"Acceleration effect? Is that like critical mass?" I asked, referring to a concept that I'd learned in physics class, whereby an atom bomb was rendered useless until it had gained enough speed and momentum, enough mass, to become highly explosive.

"Critical mass is not merely when a certain amount of people reach an awareness. It is when enough people realize what they are here to do. Looking at critical mass from a physical perspective supposes that there is a singular point that must be calibrated, a tipping point, of sorts, a point of no return. But, as the Raven has shown us, the return to the Tree of Life, the root of peace, is always awaiting us. And as people return to it on an individual level, the extraordinary starts to occur to humanity at an accelerated rate, spiraling in larger and larger circumferences until the whole world is one."

I let her words sink in, remembering the emotion I felt during my dream. The feeling of unconditional love washed over me again, that sense of ecstasy that existed while I was in that pure place of freedom. In that moment, something occurred within me. A realization came over me, as if a silent voice had whispered in my ear. I realized the meaning and essence of my life. I suddenly knew that my true purpose was to tell the story, to reveal the wisdom, to pursue peace. That I would help as many people as possible, show them that we were all connected. Tell them that the infinite cosmos existed within us all, every human, animal and plant. Reveal that the infinite cosmos was pure love.

Suddenly, an astonishing thing occurred. A dove flew down and joined the raven on the windowsill. The two birds stood together on the ledge, their wings tenderly converging. The dove angled its body towards the raven, as if leaning in for a kiss. As she did, I saw it was not a kiss at all.

The dove had passed the twig from her beak into the raven's.

CHAPTER 23

Friday morning, September 30th

Ramallah, West Bank

It was time for morning prayer, and the Chairman had his staff position him in front of his mat and adjust his chair to the lowest level. He was too old to kneel on the ground, but symbolically, he went through the motions. He did his ablutions, or rather, had his staff do them, removed his shoes, or rather, had his staff do that also, and bent forward, in prayer.

His prayer mat was a beautiful, silk *Hatchli* from Turkey, with the traditional design of candelabras along its borders. The background of the rug was woven with the finest of golden thread and embroidered on it was a tree, encircled with birds. The rug, and many like it, had been a clandestine gift, a token of support during his days of exile.

Midway through, the door to his office burst open and the Secretary-General barged in limping, relying heavily on his cane.

What a nuisance he was becoming, thought the Chairman. The Secretary-General was always opposing him, always condemning him in public. He made him look like a fool. The Chairman had considered condemning him long ago, implying failed loyalty or dual allegiances. But, the people loved him, especially the young people, and the Chairman knew he needed their support. The Secretary-General, with his blue jeans, foreign education, infidel ideals and Western values was the bane of his existence.

"I am in the middle of my prayers!" roared the Chairman.

"The security of the *Haram al-Sharif* has been breached," the Secretary-General reported, ignoring the Chairman's rage. "The guards admitted leaving their posts at the tunnel entrance to the cave in yesterday's calamity. They deemed it necessary to protect the civilians above the ground from the onslaught of soldiers."

The Chairman sat back in his chair and glowered at his young nemesis.

"Further, we have reason to believe they have found something, possibly even removed something. Yesterday's visit by that old militant was a ruse, a distraction. Obviously, a successful one."

The Chairman paused to let the words sink in. A wave of hatred swept over him. In that moment he could have killed his adversary. Instead, he performed the worst insult a man could possibly do to another man.

He threw his shoe at him.

Chapter 24

Friday morning, September 30th
Hebrew University, Jerusalem

The Old Soldier hurried across the campus to the Antiquities Department, but the archaeologist wasn't there. Looking over his shoulder, the Old Soldier ensured he wasn't being followed before making his way to the hidden lab in the basement of the university.

He found the archaeologist, who'd been in the lab all night, hunched over his work, meticulously deciphering every detail. The Sapphire tablet sat under a glass-topped table, the soft lights alternated their aim in ten second increments so as not to damage the relic.

"What is it?" The Old Soldier's voice was startlingly loud in the quiet lab.

"We can't know quite yet...I will have to run a thorough analysis." The archaeologist smiled. "But, as far as I can see, it's authentic."

"What is that cuneiform?" The Old Soldier approached the table hesitantly. He had always been fascinated by archaeology. As a child, he had fantasized about being an archaeologist and had always been passionate about antiquities. If his military career

236

had not been so glorious, so demanding, maybe he would have pursued his dream.

"Even more astonishing," responded the archaeologist. "Hard to date without thermoluminescence. See there, what looks like a triangle with the three lines under it, for instance? That is the symbol for the Tree of Life, the symbol of Asherah, the Lion Lady... signifies Temple period, even pre-Temple...but the language, the symbols used, suggests that it is much older. This is a real enigma. Whatever this artifact is, it promises to be quite revolutionary, quite revolutionary indeed." He sat back, removed his glasses and rubbed the inside corners of his eyes. He used the edge of his lab coat to wipe his glasses before putting them back on.

"How long until you have it decoded?" He was already thinking of his tactical plan.

"Well, without my colleagues' help..."

The Old Soldier bore down on him, dropping his voice to a threatening tone. "No. I told you. This must be kept completely under wraps. Only you can know of this. No one else. It is a matter of utmost secrecy."

But, the scientist, being an academic and a scholar, was not easily intimidated by the tactics of military communication. "Yes, understood, but nevertheless, without my colleagues, it may take a long time indeed. This is painstaking work to decode, authenticate, and translate."

"How long?"

"Weeks, months. It all depends..."

"Depends on what?"

"Depends on what this is."

EPILOGUE

Present day
Old City of Jerusalem

I returned to the streets of Jerusalem, surprised by how little had changed, and yet, how much had changed. Over a decade had passed since the uprising, since I'd met Sophia. I had studied, travelled, had become a mother, had been keeping the secret of the Spheres. I remembered everything that Sophia had taught me, still lived with it in every action, in every impulse, in every thought. I still explored my essence, still engaged my energy. I was aligned with my intentions; I had embraced my ideals. As gently and as often as I could, I had emancipated my ego. And she was right. I was experiencing the extraordinary in my life and my surroundings.

What was most important was that I had come to a place of forgiveness. When I forgave my father for his absence, I forgave all men. I no longer defined myself by my independence and autonomy, no longer did I need to prove my worth to the world. I let my power stem from my own intuitive wisdom. The strength of my being came from letting go and trusting myself. Trusting that every step, every thought, every emotion was exactly what it should be. Trusting that buried within me was all of the knowledge and understanding of the wise women who came before me. That I was a Story Woman and stories created freedom.

Yet, here I was in Jerusalem, looking for her to answer my one remaining question.

I found the portico that had housed my fear for so many hours.

I found the gate leading up to Sophia's apartment.

I found the blue door.

Even before I knocked, I knew.

She was not there.

The lady who answered the door was young, with a baby straddled on one hip and a few children hiding behind her, curious to see who the stranger at the door was. She hesitantly told me that she had no idea who lived in the house before her, then shuffled her children back inside and slammed the door.

I sat on the steps, a new notebook in my lap. I never saw Natalie again, nor Hanan. Not even Shai, whose number I came across years later, tucked into my old notebook, folded and forgotten. I looked down at the ring on my finger. The little earring that Ben had found that day turned out to be an inexpensive amethyst. It didn't matter to me. I had it made into a ring that I wore on my index finger. It protected me everywhere I went.

Ben had been waiting, had spent the whole night outside of the gate, right where I had left him, awaiting my return. He brought me back to Tel Aviv and I returned to be with him every chance I got. We spent the first few years of our relationship traveling the globe together, going wherever the Conduits of Consciousness were needed, wherever the scales between war and peace needed some extra weight to tip it towards the peace side. We wrote, spoke, and advocated for the pursuit of peace. We were peace. And as much as Ben adored me and I adored him, I knew that I must make my journey alone.

As for Shai, I often mistook the smiling eyes of a soldier in uniform for him and the alluring smile of a stranger would sometimes remind me of him. But, Shai was an illusion, a distant memory and a recurring dream.

The irony was that my life had become so enriched by the amount I contributed to those around me. The more I endeavored to pursue other people's freedoms, happiness and interests, the more my own freedom, happiness and interests increased. Ultimately, I realized that to give the gift to others was to receive. That then was the balance.

"Be the change you wish to see in the world," my notebook had implored.

I was. I had.

I thought of Sophia's parting words to me, "Tell the story, little bird."

"Who do I tell?" I'd asked, trying in vain to postpone my departure.

"Tell whomever will listen," she'd replied.

"What do I tell them?"

"Tell them the story of the spider, of the swallow, of the raven. Tell them that each nation on Earth holds a piece of the 'truth' puzzle, none are holding the ultimate truth. The only ultimate truth is that humanity exists as one. Tell them that all the ancient traditions gave us the guidance. The future of humanity depends on the evolution of empathy, of love for one another, and of balance."

"What if people won't change their ways?"

"You have reached a climax in your development. Your climate is in crisis, your global interdependence is so precarious, your weapons are so destructive. If humanity decides not to become empathetic, to deny compassion, then they assure the demise of your civilization. War is archaic, an obsolete model. One-sided victory is an illusion. You can no longer destroy your neighbors, for that will annihilate you. You can no longer harm your enemies, for that will inflict damage on yourself. The choice is yours to make."

"When? How will I know when to tell the story?"

"The world is at the dawn of a new awakening, a new reality. The future is one of diverse civilizations whose elements join together to develop the whole system. This diversity is the element of harmony, the element of peace. After the awakening, humanity will live at an entirely new level, enjoying higher kinds of awareness, yet not in conflict with the spiritual teachings of the world. There will be harmony between all the world's beliefs."

"People won't believe me," I had argued.

"They do not have to believe you. The new paradigm of reality is not conducive to the culture of fear that we have been living in. For many centuries, the accepted doctrines were based out of necessity for the shaping of society. We lived completely ignorant of many truths of our natures. That was simply part of the evolution of the race. The world was not ready for these truths to come out yet."

"When will it be the right time?" I'd asked.

"To live inside time is different than to live next to it. There will be many signs, but one will speak to you directly. Only you will know when the time is right to reveal the secrets, for you too are a Story Woman."

"How will I know? What will be the sign?" I had asked her.

"When the people develop an interest, it is always the first sign. When people start to ask questions, to have a hunger, a curiosity, that is when the old paradigms can fall and new understandings can replace them. When people are returning to a fascination of the power within, when they are willing to fight to replace the old realities with new realities, that is when you will know."

In the years that have passed, I searched for the clues, for the "signs." There were many signs throughout the years that led me to think the time was right, that people were ready.

When the twin towers were attacked by religious fundamentalists, intent on terrorizing the world in the name of their beliefs.

When the Old Soldier inexplicably suffered a brain aneurism, rendering him in a perpetual coma.

When the Chairman renewed his efforts at peace negotiations, went insane, and then abruptly died.

When the Iranian government created a rocket, designed to carry long-range missiles, named the Simorgh.

When the mysterious white ravens were spotted off the Pacific coast.

When the global financial systems collapsed.

When ordinary people were rallying in the streets, fighting for change.

When uprising after uprising toppled hierarchal regimes.

When the Secretary-General, my father, was assassinated.

There seemed to be a myriad of signs to choose from. Yet, there I was, more than a decade later, back in the streets of Jerusalem, still searching for the ultimate sign.

I was about to get up to leave, and that's when I saw it...

There, on the top of the gate sat the *bulbul.*

And I knew.

The time had come.

APPRECIATION

The inspiration to write this book came from many known and unknown sources, my appreciation flows abundantly to both.

I was inspired by the Dalai Lama, who set me on this path, with his infamous prophecy that "the world will be changed by the Western Woman." Thank you for that moment of epiphany. I am doing my part.

To the initial readers of this book, in its various stages of incarnation, your words of encouragement and support have been integral to the growth of this story. Thank you Talia Novik, Tanya Freedman, Gwendolyn Elliot and A.R. White.

Thank you to Samantha Stroh-Bailey for your keen eyes and brilliant insights. You are an extraordinary editor and endless means of encouragement.

Deep gratitude goes to Sabaina Malik for being a force in the rise of a tribe of authors, of which I am proud to call myself one of.

To the incomparable website and book cover designer, Lucinda Kinch, your artistry is only surpassed by the radiance of your being. It has been a true pleasure to work with you.

Thank you to the many women and men in my many

communities, who supported this project in seen and unseen ways. I honor you and all you have contributed to this endeavor.

Mostly, my appreciation goes to my soul mate Daniel, for letting me fly and for being a loving nest to land in. My heart is full.

ABOUT THE AUTHOR

EM Richter is a storyteller, poet, peacemaker, philosopher, and an ecstatic dancer. She began her academic studies in Philosophy and Anthropology, and continued in a passionate pursuit of esoteric mysticism and ancient cultures.

Trained as a Peace Ambassador and an Agent for Conscious Evolution, EM is part of a growing community of sacred activists.

EM lives in Toronto with her family.

The Secret of the Storyteller is her debut novel.

Visit her at www.emrichter.com

CPSIA information can be obtained at www.ICGtesting.com
Printed in the USA
LVOW05s1043090114

368628LV00001B/2/P